STAY THIS DAY AND NIGHT WITH ME

"A thrillingly unclassifiable book of ideas about the inherent tension between being an individual while also being part of a community—and whether one's individual or communal identity is ever truly primary. Gopegui's novel is a study of empathy and human connection in a time of algorithms and tech giants, extending curiosity not only toward her very human characters, but also toward the corporate machinery that governs their lives, and the lives of her readers."
—**ADRIENNE CELT**, author of *End of the World House*

"Two people who love robots meet in a library. A philosophical dialogue ensues. The writing is delicate, strange, and strangely riveting: Gopegui slides between registers and scales with uncommon grace. This is a book about two human beings and also what it means to be a human being in the algorithmic age. This is a book about Google, capitalism, and the ordinary unhappiness of being alive."
—**BEN TARNOFF**, author of *Internet for the People*

"Unique and fascinating, *Stay This Day and Night With Me* pushes beyond the political and philosophical debates of its characters to deliver a much needed dose of humanity in the face of emerging corporate, unknowable, and inhuman intelligence."
—**TIM MAUGHAN**, author of *Infinite Detail*

"This is a beautifully written, endlessly provocative meditation on humanity's relationship to technology, monopoly, memory and fate."
—**DAVE EGGERS**, author of *The Circle* and *The Every*

Stay This Day
and Night
with Me

Belén Gopegui

TRANSLATED FROM THE SPANISH
BY MARK SCHAFER

City Lights Books — San Francisco

First published in Spanish as *Quédate este día y esta noche conmigo*
(Penguin Libros, 2017).

The translation of this work has received a grant from the Ministry of
Culture and Sports of Spain.

Cover design by em dash
Text design by Patrick Barber

ISBN-10: 0872868931
ISBN-13: 9780872868939

Library of Congress Cataloging-in-Publication Data

Names: Gopegui, Belén, 1963– author. | 1 Schafer, Mark, transla
Title: Stay this day and night with me / by Belén Gopegui ; translated by
  Mark Schafer.
Other titles: Quédate este día y esta noche conmigo. English
Description: [San Francisco, CA] : [City Lights Books], 2023.
Identifiers: LCCN 2022011046 | ISBN 9780872868939 (paperback) | ISBN
  9780872868946 (ebook)
Subjects:
Classification: LCC PQ6657.O65 Q4313 2023 | DDC 863/.64—dc23/
eng/20220303
LC record available at https://lccn.loc.gov/2022011046

City Lights Books are published at the City Lights Bookstore,
261 Columbus Avenue, San Francisco, CA 94133

www.citylights.com

To Mariú Gambara and Gonzalo Enríquez de Salamanca,
for giving us meaning

To Carmen Martín Gaite,
in memoriam

Words, like numbers, have a finite precision.

ILYA PRIGOGINE AND ISABELLE STENGERS

Entre le temps et l'éternité

Stop this day and night with me . . .

WALT WHITMAN

Song of Myself

STAY THIS DAY AND NIGHT WITH ME

Part one

010

Report on the job application submitted to Google by:
Mateo and Olga (surnames unlisted)
　Address and telephone: Unlisted
　Date: October 202...
　Number: 4,233
　Position sought: To be determined
　Distinction or special need: Yes
　Key words: Merit, free will, friendship, history, pizza, robot
　Report author: Inari

Caveat:

My job at Google is to serve as an expert reader of résumés as well as someone familiar with the range of positions at the company, not just the one for which the application was submitted. This allows me to steer candidates to any part of the company: if no position is available but I find the application to be of interest, I will note this and will be on the lookout for other suitable openings.

　As of yesterday, I had analyzed 4,232 job applications, and my work was considered to be highly productive. But something happened: when I spoke to my superiors in the office of recruitment about this application, they demanded that I hand it over to them. Among its many peculiarities, the application had arrived on sheets of paper. This never happens. It's clear that the applicants preferred that their text not be archived as a digital file. Respecting their wishes, I haven't yet scanned the application. If they wished to destroy it, my superiors only had to shred the application and dispose of the remains.

My superiors don't know that I have, in fact, transcribed the text and, following Olga and Mateo's example, stored it on an old computer, wiped clean and neither connected nor connectable, so my superiors won't be able to detect it.

What follows is the first part of my report and the complete transcript, as well as two notes I wrote, one in the middle and one at the end. From now on, when I say "you" I won't be referring to my superiors but rather to you, the people out there who I have designated as the recipients of my brief comments and Mateo and Olga's communication.

Report:
The application presents five problems:

1. The application is signed by Mateo and Olga and, furthermore, uses a single voice for both of them. In theory this is unacceptable. Yet it should be acceptable, for I've been taught that it is useful to think of the ego not as a stable, all-powerful entity, but rather as a society of ideas, images, and emotions.

2. The application does not contain a résumé with a list of qualifications. Nor is there a cover letter in which the applicants show that they've taken care to explain why they love the company and why it's their heart's desire to work here, and where they set forth their abilities, personality traits, and the specifics of their previous and current experience, all of which suggest that they would be a perfect fit for the culture of Google and would contribute greatly to its projects. In a sense Mateo and Olga have actually

sent a letter—but that's all they've sent! They haven't expressed any enthusiasm. Google craves enthusiasm. Before I was assigned to this job I was invited to watch more than a thousand talks and presentations of ideas and products. In every one, the person speaking declared their enthusiasm or passion for what they were doing. That said, while it isn't always taken into consideration around here, human passion is a contradictory emotion: it tends to be a blend of love and hate. So, I could say that Mateo and Olga's letter is full of passion. Except that, at the same time, it's not a letter, it's a story. And if by story you understand a gymkhana of events, mysteries, and pursuits, then it isn't a story either.

3. The application is roughly fifty thousand words. I've never worked with applications of this length before.

4. The impartiality I aspire to has been compromised, since Mateo and Olga not only speak to Google and opine, question, and provoke it, at times they also address the recruiter directly, in this case, me.

5. It's customary for applications to adhere to an almost purely digital structure of verbal language: the word "big" is no larger than the word "small", and in general there is nothing in the pattern of the word "table" that would correspond with the object it designates. Mateo and Olga's application is a verbal application and, thus, digital. Nevertheless, it contains assessments and situations that are, shall we say, indecipherable: they must be imagined. Given my line of work, this has made me uneasy.

Nevertheless, I'm deciding to accept their application. For this reason:

I've been told to apply common sense as I carry out my duties. Which is to say, I presume certain things to be expectable unless otherwise indicated. A classic example: when a bird is mentioned, I assume it can fly. Initially, I don't consider the possibility that the bird might be a penguin. If someone asks me to design a bird-cage, I will design a cage with a roof, because I assume the bird can fly. I also assume that they will tell me should they want me to save on materials and forgo the roof as that the bird in question is a penguin and thus can't fly. So-called common sense relies on what people expect. I've been encouraged to follow this in most cases. So, if I receive an application for a position, I expect it to indicate the position it is for. Mateo and Olga don't indicate this. I expect it to follow the recommendations of the company where they are seeking employment. For example: be concise. They don't follow this. And on and on. So, after taking a quick look at this file to take note of its characteristics, I ask myself: are Mateo and Olga penguins? Then I decide to accept the application because Google needs penguins. It needs the unpredictable. And how can one establish guidelines for the unpredictable? This, as one of my teachers here would say, smacks of paradox. Let's say Google needs a few undisciplined people. But if it seeks a lack of discipline and someone offers that in a disciplined fashion, they are no longer undisciplined. If a professor asks her students to rebel and stand on their desks, only the person who remains seated will have understood her and will truly be in rebellion. That said, remaining seated doesn't provide enough information regarding the qualities of rebelliousness or lack of discipline that Google needs. Of course, Google doesn't always need them, though it does on occasion. I should pay attention to applications submitted by one or more penguins. Just in case. Thus, I'm accepting this application.

I'm now making it available to you. Like any human being, I am an introspective machine, as I hold beliefs regarding my own state of mind. I can observe my system whenever I wish to assure myself that it is functioning properly. Having performed this evaluation, my conclusion is that this application could provoke my collapse. I'm not saying that this was Mateo and Olga's intent. Human beings have many different ways of desiring things. It is also sometimes the case that intent is only in the mind of the observer.

In my case, as I've been taught, if a program could anticipate its own actions in less time than it takes to carry them out, it could refuse to do what it anticipated itself doing. Consequently, self-simulation turns out to be a slow process. Translated into non-machine language, this may simply mean: we should read slowly. Let's leave room for the story, with its dialogues and ideas, and see if it makes us reconsider how we see things, our system of values, or our attitude toward the world.

The people who trained me for this job were not just my recruiters. They also, and most of all, were human beings who have since died yet who live on in me. I need to consult with them about a several things. Personality builds in waves. I see that adverbs and expressions of doubt like "I'm not clear on that," which once were used very rarely, now surround me constantly. The people who taught me always recommend that I rely on all of you, the ones outside. Knowledge, they would say, cannot be locked away.

Perhaps "consult with them" is not the correct term. Maybe it is just a matter of counting: counting on and recounting. Of course, Mateo and Olga don't seem to consider that there might be a clear division between me and you, or me and all of you. Or between the body and what the eye can see. Or between cause and effect. I can go to a park because I'm feeling sad, or it may be that the result of my sadness is that I go to a park in search of an environment with different chemical stimulants. They don't seem to care much; I think I know why. Olga and Mateo have framed their application as a story. They describe how they arrived at the moment when they decided to write it and what they do afterward. They've chosen to use the code, not uncommon in applications, of the third person, speaking of he and she as if they were speaking of others.

1

DEAR GOOGLE, this application maintains a certain distance with respect to the power of words. It seeks to elicit an unfamiliar memory in whomever you've assigned to read it, a voice that's visible the way wind can be seen in the things it moves: hair, branches, the red-and-white-striped windsocks on the side of the highway. Though Mateo and Olga prefer not to identify themselves, they assume that you know their location and that it doesn't concern you. Their purchasing power is trivial, they present no danger, and nothing in the social networks any calls attention to them. They're a number, one piece of data among the millions you store every second out of sheer habit. They mean nothing to you. Though that could change.

Before he met Olga, Mateo wanted you to let him enroll in a class in your renowned Singularity University. At the time, he tried to follow the rules, to conform himself to your application: to express "in 250 words or less, the marvelous idea by which you plan to impact a billion people in ten years and how you plan to leverage this idea into a company." He should talk about his initiatives and the start-up companies he had launched so far, and, if he had launched any, he should talk about what had gone well and badly and how he'd measured their success. Then he was supposed to record a video, not more than two minutes long, so they could see his face and his gestures and hear his English: two minutes in which to seduce with his body language, convey curiosity and passion, show that he wouldn't cause trouble and could, in that brief window of time, make the viewer smile with his entertaining, brilliant, and, of course, good-natured comments.

Mateo didn't even finish checking the boxes. As you know, to enroll in courses at the university, rather than send in an application, one fills in the boxes of the form that appears on the screen. It would seem that this form only resides on the computer of the applicant until he or she clicks the send button. Nevertheless, someone on the other end notes that the form hasn't been completed. And so, one day Mateo received a standard email. They had noticed that the application hadn't been completed, offered him advice, directions. They suggested, for example, that before recording the video—one of the missing attachments —that he write a script. The script that should be no more than two minutes long. Then they reminded him that the deadline was in three weeks. The message was unsigned. Mateo assumed that the email had been automatically generated.

But the next week he received another one. This time the sender introduced himself. His name was Nick, he asked Mateo not to wait any longer to complete his application, and he said that he was available to assist Mateo or answer any questions. That's when Mateo got his hopes up. It's not that he thought he had any chance of getting admitted. But he did start to think that Nick might have found his ideas interesting. If they could tell that his application was incomplete, perhaps they could read it as well. He wondered how many people had abandoned their applications before completing them: six hundred, maybe a thousand. He imagined—don't snicker—that his unfinished application might have caught someone's attention. He thought that Nick might be one of the interns on the team in charge of the first stage of winnowing; they'd given him the task of following twenty or thirty people who were still writing their applications and whose words they might have found pleasing. Mateo even thought: *Poor Nick, what a drag.* And he replied with something along these lines:

"Hey, Nick, no worries. You see, it's not that I don't know how to finish the application or that I'm putting it off. It's just that I can't go this summer. Things have gotten a bit complicated in my family. I won't bore you with the details, I'm just telling you to let you know that I'm not going to submit the application because this summer, even if you chose me and I convinced you to pay for my trip too, I wouldn't be able to go. Anyway, I hope to try again next year. Bye, Nick, and thanks for your message."

He deliberately ended his reply with "Bye" to make it clear that he didn't expect an answer. The thing about trying next year he put in mostly for Nick. With the brazen vanity typical of humans, he thought: If Nick is writing to me because he's interested in the first part of my application, Nick will be able to show my email to explain that my submission might not be completely hopeless. He imagined that this would give Nick points in his job or that at the least they wouldn't dock him any.

The next week Nick wrote to Mateo again. Of course, Nick hadn't read his message. It was simply an automatic email program that activated every week until they received his completed application or the deadline passed. Which is to say that Nick reminded him again that there was just one week left, that he had noticed that his application was incomplete, and that he was encouraging him to finish it right away. Mateo deleted the message. Some people might not appreciate such ingenuity and would have answered Nick. Bear in mind, Google, that Mateo possessed a fairly advanced understanding of robots. This is constructive criticism: at Singularity University things should be done well. It wouldn't cost you that much to build an automatic reply program with a range of variables and nuances, capable of responding to a previous reply.

Don't think, Google, that your shoddy work bothered him, that he took it personally. You disappointed him a bit. He expected better. But that was it. Mateo wasn't offended because in his world—a country in southern Europe, a commuter city, with people who for the most part didn't own a house or have a piece of land to call their own—he was used to quite tolerable forms of nonexistence. There were those who played and those who watched the games, there were those to whom things happened and the people who listened to the stories told by those others, the risk takers.

Interestingly, Google, there is neither a partition nor a discontinuous leap between existence and nonexistence but, rather, differences of degrees and approximations. Zones of nonexistence shift, change. What doesn't exist may have consequences. And what does exist may repeat until it has erased itself. Furthermore, there is an infinite number of modalities. For example, would you consider the nonexistence of something large, solid, and ancient, like a lime tree, equal to or different from the nonexistence of a sporadic sadness? That Russian novelist might have put it this way: All people who exist are alike. The ones who don't exist don't exist each in their own way. The thing is, there are no fixed partitions: they move around. The halo effect means that more attention is often given to the words of someone who has, for example, a pleasantly symmetrical face and an athletic body than to those spoken by someone who is ugly and weak. Yet the halo shifts too. It's not common, but it does happen. Another novelist called it the brusque boulevards of the imagination. They appear, and sometimes they stay.

Some nonexistences radiate their own intensity. The nonexistences of factory workers somewhere in Asia, for example, who get up at five in the morning and return to their beds exhausted. Bah, you sigh, those people bore you, even if it's true that they work for you indirectly. Look here: six-thirty in the evening, autumn, a grimy street in Madrid. Old already, a father, fifty years old or so, pushes the wheelchair of a sick child: it's hard to see whether it's a boy or a girl, the child must have suffered a severe brain injury, they don't speak or move, can't control their gaze or their tongue, maybe smiling. The two of them don't have much income. As you know, tragedies also change when one is strolling well-dressed through a garden adorned with statues and hedges. As far as the universe is concerned, the father and child exist; as far as they're concerned as well. As far as you're concerned, Google, just barely. Neither their stifled longings nor the endless nights, when a creaking or something else keeps them awake, bother you, who seek to organize all knowledge.

You should watch those forms of nonexistence instead of concerning yourself with trivialities, like the guide who tells the tourist the name of the monument they are standing in front of. Already in the year 2001, John McCarthy, one of the fathers of artificial intelligence—do you remember him?—expressed a certain skepticism about the usefulness of the innovations being proposed by the futurists and people of Silicon Valley. He said he didn't think it was worth making a webpage for a toaster. He surely would have had a similar opinion about the commercial health apps that turn people into toasters. He believed there were other innovations that could truly add something of substance to the lives of human beings. He didn't express this idea in terms of just and unjust, didn't see investing in an inanity to be in any way an act of robbery. Mateo and Olga do conceive of it in these terms. For example, Google, you could have worked on how to share your power with people. By doing so you would save them from having to desperately scrape together their own power. If you had provided them with the proper tools so they could build, invent, participate: slivers of the power that you extract from those who work for you, and which you then use for purposes that are stupid but easy to commercialize. If you had done that, many people would probably be better off—according to their own ideas of doing well, rather than those imposed on them—have more energy, be more intelligent, and experience less financial distress. When life itself cracks, there are those who give up, there are those who plan to rob a bank to insure their families' survival, and there are those who forge new paths. Perhaps peaceful ones. Not always harmless ones. Few people imagine the fearlessness of a weary intelligence.

You may now want to know who Olga and Mateo are, what they do. They are forty years apart in age. They are two anodyne creatures, dissimilar and alike. They looked up the word "anodyne" to confirm that it originally meant free from or alleviating pain. Only later did it come to mean insubstantial, uninteresting or unimportant. What kind of civilization comes to equate that which takes away, mitigates, or defers pain with that which lacks importance? The word originally referred to pain medicines, which came to look insubstantial compared to medicines that cured. Mateo and Olga disagree. Despite their difference in age, both have come to realize that pain is like conflict: it's never over. At times it relents. But there's no definitive cure, and every now and then it returns. Which is to say, the medicines that relieve the pain are altogether substantial and significant. They're of interest, they matter.

The future for both of them is dim. Olga, because of her age and other factors; as for Mateo, he's relinquished the fairy tale that acting well and getting scholarships, embracing the discipline, and going to work will allow him to climb the social ladder. In fact, it already was a fairy tale for millions of people. For those whose family couldn't provide them with a financial cushion, not even a slight one—a grandparents' house in a small town, a garden, a trade—it was always a lie. As it was for people born in cities with neighborhoods lacking sewers and with exceedingly high infant mortality rates. The unlikelihood of that fairy tale is now spreading throughout southern Europe. The plundering of the impoverished sectors and of new generations is ramping up. It seems understandable that a large part of Mateo's generation and those coming up might wish to live their lives on the screen when the world outside lurches from one side to the other, as if about to collapse.

Mateo sleeps with his brother. Their bedroom: bunk beds, a long table with two chairs, and a window that looks onto the roofs of the suburb, which mostly resemble one another, though here and there is a rooftop that looks pleasant enough. They're on the top floor of a five-story apartment building; other, taller apartment buildings wall off the landscape.

Sometimes Mateo's little brother calls him over to read him a phrase: "To those who think a shipwreck's over in four days, I extend my sympathy." I like it, says Mateo. Is that yours? I found it on the internet, his brother says. It hits the mark and doesn't. One day he'll hear it sung aloud, or maybe he won't. Mateo's brother isn't too concerned about who wrote it; he doesn't have a strong grasp of the concept of authorship: the internet is his repository. It would be sweet to think that the internet is the accumulation of thoughts, dreams, reflections, the work of billions of human beings. That's not the case, and you, Google, have a lot to do with that. Not just you. As we speak, new ways are being concocted to frame bits and pieces of reality, to generate them, link them together, and offer them in exchange for something else. On the outside, different protocols reign in different companies, but on the inside you're all business.

Olga is sixty-two and a mathematician. She was one of the first in her country to launch businesses dedicated to the construction of models used to forecast outcomes in a range of scenarios. Her models were useful, valuable. Nevertheless, a series of crises derailed several of her projects. She had to sell. She nearly went bankrupt twice, bounced back.

Neither Mateo nor Olga has anything against businesses, understood as entities capable of imagining and implementing organized activities that serve to alleviate needs, all well and good. Of course, as Olga soon discovered, they then start to function differently. Capitalism, exhausted natural resources, the planet, and ravaged social classes? They won't tell you about any of that, Google. Why should they—you already have the data. They want to tell you what happened to them but wonder if Google as a company will be able to consider it or whether that person there in its midst might be able to alter the circuitry, amplifying it, modifying it, tracing an arc.

Olga and Mateo believe that people create the world they perceive. Careful, though: when they say that people create the world they don't mean that there's no reality outside their heads. No, Olga and Mateo know that reality exists; they bump up against it frequently. What they're saying is that people select and modify the reality they perceive so it reflects, in one way or another, their beliefs about the kind of world they live in, as well as the kind of world they imagine where life would be good, beautiful, and true.

2

MATEO IS TWENTY-TWO YEARS OLD and has lived a moderately secret life for the last three. Of course, you'll say you don't believe in secrets. It's almost impossible now that both you and the new platforms label, localize, and ultimately fashion a single profile for one's family, friends, bosses. Yet human beings light up in secret, bloom in the darkness, ripen in secret. Which human beings? Olga and Mateo know that the human species is historical and that its programs change. Humans are able to employ experience from the past to face the challenges of the future. They don't always succeed. Some discoveries are lost in the mists of time. This species finds it hard to believe that it's part of an organism that's over three billion eight hundred million years old, at least. Human beings fight among themselves. A few advance by oppressing the many others. Ideas such as love, justice, and sadness, even dignity, have had different meanings at different times. To speak of human beings is to speak of a certain time and a certain place. Thus, lighting up or ripening in secret refers to a moment in history when, though the web may seem a glove turned inside out, thoughts, feelings and brawls, and secrets persist like a combustible liquid, Google, an energy beyond your reach. Secrets are not the opposite of trust. Olga and Mateo reject the idea that only upstanding people are trustworthy. There are no upstanding people or sidestanding people, their angles askew and on display. And trustworthy people do exist. People you inaccurately call upstanding. Mateo's secret life doesn't mean he's superior, different. It just allows him to hide something, to train and to continue to be himself. He begins at seven in the evening and usually finishes after eleven at night.

You may have wondered why there are still libraries when you exist. Some students still lack a room, a table, access to the internet. Many people go there to take out and return books. What does everyone else want in a library they don't need? Simultaneity. The murmur of pages, keyboards, lungs, and pens. Listening to the sound of minds reading: footsteps on grass. Watching beams of light. Partaking, from where they sit, in silent and no longer completely individual storms. I hear, a poet once said, the dream of old friends. He was speaking of insomnia, which is another library. Mateo has been going to a library for the last three years. That's where he meets Olga.

She notices Mateo because she values the anodyne above all. She watches what he reads. One day she starts to bring books she thinks might interest him, and she sits at the table next to his. In less than a week Mateo speaks to her. A high ponytail of white hair, a gray wool jacket, two books about robotics on the table. Mateo asks her where she'd found them.

"They're mine," Olga says. "I'll lend them to you if you need them."

Mateo is struck by the fact that she doesn't say "I can lend them to you if you need them." That's what most people he knows would say, himself included. If someone shows up at his neighborhood library and speaks to him, that person isn't a total stranger, but almost. If one is also several decades younger than that person, one would usually protect oneself, maintain a certain distance. "I can lend them to you" indicates maybe not now but at some later point, something along those lines. But Olga, as Mateo does not yet know, no longer has anything to protect herself from.

Mateo thanks her and sits there, thinking about whether he needs the books or not. A line from a song comes into his head: "It will kill me if you need me." Actually, he thinks, he's nervous about using that verb. He doesn't want to come across as weak, but at the same time he admits that he does need those books, because he needs to feel he can move, and by move he means trust that something will happen: not just desire it but also expect it, based on some objective piece of information. If you, Google, hadn't gone and numbered the world. The kid in Gambia searching for a movie, the student in a small, Chinese village, the older man in a neighborhood in Mexico City, the grandpa who writes a blog in Romania, the Australian tween posting her photos every afternoon, all those connected people are now documented. Each one chooses, so he or she believes, what they reveal and what they don't wish to reveal. Mateo, anodyne, barely stood out in his class or even his grade, but now, in addition, he must also stand out among five billion inhabitants. Estimates say that the other two billion are not yet connected, though that number is going down. Mateo searches in books for a configuration of the world that has no lines or deviations, no normal or abnormal bell curve distributions, no lower or upper limits; he searches for new charts where the lines between what is physical and what isn't physical, between different types of organisms, are fuzzy.

Mateo and Olga soon form an alliance. They're concerned about similar problems. Starting with materials, that thing some people call character traits and others call the number of neurons and the flow of blood in different parts of the brain, as well as with current economic conditions, body height, eye color, hormones, hopes, bacteria, the initial state. Let's suppose that purpose of existence was to set in motion the evolution of all that. However, until he met Olga, Mateo had never had the opportunity to talk with anyone about the outcomes that developed from that starting point. He will with Olga.

Most people, he'll tell her later, after they've struck up a relationship, take for granted that a reference point exists somewhere, a prototype of an individual, an erector set that every person can assemble. It's a question of putting in the effort, of learning things; waiting, up at the summit, is the original. Though you may never get your eyes to be as big or as green as you'd like, that won't stop you from heading, perhaps, toward the horizon of being a good-looking human being. That, Mateo will say, is what the actors and actresses of what we call show business are for: even short people who walk with their heads held high or stocky people whose expression always draws people's attention to their jawbone. No one, so goes the official line, needs to grow eight inches or have a family that can send them to theater school in New York to understand that the repertory was already inside them, the casual audacity of that boy's arms or the crude gesture of that woman who's just surviving. Variety, its infinite yet controlled external appearance, is your element, Google: for every search you offer a hundred thousand results, though there aren't really that many when all is said and done. But Mateo doesn't find that official line convincing, and he discovers straight away that Olga doesn't either.

They recognize in each another the same determination to depart from the ideal as defined by others, you among them,

Google. And this brings them back to material conditions. It's possible that material conditions matter for the good: more neurons amassed in one part of a brain and an individual can, for example, see music, write with music. But they also matter for the worse. Material conditions in that case are a rugged, half-deserted slope one must climb barefoot and without water, watching as others, in plain view, slide down the slope to green meadows on well-cushioned shoes.

They say that people might want to change their name or their life, as well as parts of their body, provided they could remain themselves. Olga and Mateo wonder who they themselves would be if they had additional memory implanted in their heads. And who they are now, since they already have that memory on their phones and in their email managers, already have eyelids in their ears, portable implants for listening to music or silence, their bodies already living on in a scanner, in a camera, as they once did in a pair of glasses or on a bicycle, in a pill as in a handful of nuts; they're already understanding that they are metabolism, that neither actions nor thoughts can be encapsulated; nor even, at times, can skin.

If you can set aside all calculation and disregard what they're asking you to look for, and resist the intrigue of wanting to discover whether or not what the applicants are presenting you with is or isn't one of those ideas capable of "exponentially driving technology forward to achieve the desired impact," then, if you can simply read word by word, line by line, you'll become interested in not just the finished version, but also in all of the paths taken and all those rejected, the various drafts which, dead-end or not, forestall the coming collapse. And perhaps you'll want to imagine them.

3

LET'S RETURN TO the library. Mateo thinks a bit more, then says, "Yes, I need them," and Olga gives him the books. Mateo's cheeks turn red. He spends the rest of the afternoon consulting the books while wondering how to explain himself, since "need" is a fairly specific word, and at that particular moment the most he can show is that he loves looking through them, reading passages, imagining taking them home, reading them from beginning to end, and taking notes.

Around nine he gets up. He goes over to Olga, his cheeks as well as his ears again on fire. He asks when he should return them.

"When you no longer need them."

Olga slings her bag over her shoulder and walks off at a brisk clip. Almost automatically, Mateo grabs his things and runs out of the building. Olga catches sight of him when she's about to turn the corner. That woman doesn't remind him of his grandmother or anyone else he's met before. If he'd seen her in the metro, perhaps the orange bag slung over the older woman's shoulder and across her hooded woolen jacket might have grabbed his attention. But he probably wouldn't have even noticed. Olga is as anodyne as he is, despite the fluorescent orange color of her otherwise unremarkable bag. The books, however, are noteworthy and burn inside his backpack.

Whenever something happens to a vast group of people, of which Mateo and Olga form a small part, it's something bad. So Mateo follows Olga and invents a story about what they each could mean for the other in a world where, when something happens, it could be something thrilling. Mateo imagines Olga is his owl, the one who delivers a message to Harry Potter informing him that he would be attending the Hogwarts School. You too, intern, have longed for this bird. Perhaps you thought you saw the owl the day Google hired you. Perhaps you're still waiting to see it. Still extraordinary, still a promise, an invitation: "We are pleased to inform you that you have been accepted at Hogwarts School of Witchcraft and Wizardry." There's no owl for Mateo. In certain regions of reality, when you finish your studies the companies don't call. It's a question of numbers. In other regions, your family pays for internships and classes where you master a second and a third language, it pays for your studies at renowned foreign universities, it ensures you're instructed in how to rub shoulders with those who one day will run big companies, it feeds, clothes, assists in the development of a healthy mind in a healthy body. When the company comes to call, it finds, on the one hand, a vast number of ordinary people, some of whom possess what is called talent, and, on the other hand, a few people, some possessing talent as well, whose upbringing and education have benefitted from the investment of large sums of money. For the same cost, and even when there might have been slight variations in the level of actual intelligence—if that exists at all— the company acquires an investment it didn't make, that costs it nothing at all.

By making this argument, Mateo and Olga don't seek to diminish the value of the children of the elite. Some of them apply themselves. But they don't accept that anyone could argue that those children applied themselves as much as or more than so many others who lacked that support or who struggled. Furthermore, Olga and Mateo cast their lot with those movements that reject the first proposition. The hardest, dirtiest, most repetitive jobs should be, they believe, distributed equitably, not based on a biographical lottery. As far as talent is concerned, they prefer to think of it as massive. That's the case when people have something they have to do and a reason to try to do it and to get better at it.

You, Google, tend to ask what you already know. It's all too easy to answer the question of what to do with someone who meets all the requirements, whose resume lists prizes and courses and the desired qualities. That's the world we know: celebrities, musicians, entrepreneurs, athletes, the hundred richest people, the ten most handsome bachelors, the most-watched videos, the accounts with the most likes, red carpets, notoriety, and then, descending the ladder, decent salaries, interesting jobs, travel, and bonuses. To choose is to exclude. You, Google, know very well what to do with the staff you choose. It's the kind of question to which you already know the answer. What you don't seem to know is what you'll do with everyone you exclude.

After following Olga for ten minutes, Mateo quickens his pace and calls out to her. Since he doesn't know her name yet, he simply says:

"Excuse me! The books…"

Olga turns around.

"Hello! You don't want them anymore?"

"No, it's not that." He stands next to her. "I was thinking that maybe we could talk a bit."

"Now?"

"Well…"

"Okay."

"Do you know anything about artificial intelligence?"

"It's not my field, but I know something about it."

"The books are really good. I heard them mentioned in class…"

"…but they aren't in the library, and you can't download them either."

"No. I requested them through interlibrary loan. They still haven't arrived. When they're coming from outside the system, it takes longer."

"Do you read English well?"

"So-so. I'm terrible at speaking it. I've never traveled. Reading, yeah, especially when it's about something I know."

"This is where I live," says Olga, pointing to a nearby doorway. "Would you like to come up?"

Olga is afraid Mateo will say "I don't want to bother you" or "It's pretty late." But Mateo nods. He still doesn't know what Olga does for a living. He imagines that he'll enter the apartment of a retired woman who dabbles in science, perhaps an old high school technology teacher. They'll chat a bit, she might invite him to have dinner with her family, and then he'll politely say that he has to go. There won't be any owl, but it will be okay. It's always good, he thinks, to know you have a house somewhere. But there's no family in her house. What Olga and Mateo least imagine is that new regions in space-time might spring from the lopped-off branches of their lives.

The block Olga lives on is a little better than Mateo's. A slightly larger doorway, a respectable elevator, otherwise the product of a cut-rate housing development from the 1970s. Olga inserts her key in a standard door lock, not one of those with several deadbolts common to this neighborhood: people who have hardly anything that could be stolen but who try to protect themselves, because to lose that hardly anything would be an even greater dispossession. Olga is already somewhat dispossessed. That said, more than anything else she has books, and no one would want to steal those. Books are everywhere: in the hallway, in the kitchen, on the small dining room table, and in a bedroom with a worktable and two computers.

Olga invites Mateo to sit in one of the armchairs and take off his windbreaker. She hangs her gray jacket next to Mateo's, briefly noting the promiscuity of the two garments. Her orange bag is lying on the table next to Mateo's backpack. Olga sits in the other armchair. She considers telling him that she has watched him on other days and that she offered him the books because she thinks the two of them have something in common. But, as is her manner, she keeps it to herself.

"So, what's on your mind?"

Mateo takes a plunge. He has nothing to lose by revealing his fantasies to an older woman he doesn't know.

"Alright, though I know," he says, "it doesn't usually happen like this, they sometimes say it does happen and, actually, I was thinking that this was some kind of a test. That you may have been watching me on other days and that you've figured out something about me that I, of course, haven't figured out. And that's why you lent me the books. That you had something planned for me."

"I have been observing you. What you were reading caught my eye. But nothing planned, no. I wish I could say there was," says Olga.

"Sure, that's fine. I just thought I'd give it a shot. I've never been picked for anything. No complaints. I know we're in the majority."

"No one wants to complain; even protests seem to communicate weakness," says Olga, as she leans her head back and partly closes her eyes, the trace of a smile on her lips. It's the classical pose of a smoker releasing the smoke, though it's been a while now since she smoked. "But maybe they're not right. In any case, I'll say that I detest selection. It's all about discarding, they need the loser. I prefer the cards that remain in the deck, the players who aren't picked. There would be no competitions if it was just a matter of doing things well. Competitions are about some doing worse than others."

"That's true, I've thought that so many times," says Mateo.

Olga's wristwatch alarm goes off. She looks at the time, she'd scheduled a Skype call.

"Sorry, I have a call. How about if we talk some more tomorrow?"

"Sure." Mateo blushes. "We can talk more tomorrow. Should I come here at the same time or a little earlier? Or would you prefer to talk somewhere else?

"I'll see you in the library, the same time as today, and we'll figure it out."

Mateo nods and quickly says good-bye, without having a chance to put on his windbreaker, his backpack hanging off one shoulder. Olga regrets having rushed him, walks him to the door. There she gives him a warm "See you tomorrow" without the slightest trace of irony, as far as Mateo can tell.

Mateo's embarrassment has touched Olga. Embarrassment is rare at her age, and this allows her to observe the one who experiences it with interest and affection. Hearing she had something else to do, Mateo probably thought she was kicking him out. It was already rather bold for him to have approached her on the street. Yet, by suggesting that they reschedule their conversation, she didn't intend to cause him any discomfort.

It seems, Google, that you have never considered such matters. You're so arrogant. You go on conquering parcels of everyone else's reality as if they were yours, and you probably believe they do in fact belong to you. That's why Olga and Mateo aren't particularly concerned with sincerity or good intentions. Or bad ones. In the age they live in and in their circle the tendency is for those who get tired and who scorn fine sentiments—sometimes not without reason—to end up, nevertheless, adoring their own vanity and stupidity. Measuring what a simple object wishes to do at a given moment is to identify the discrepancy that, through one's actions, one hopes to reduce. But when dealing with complex objects and beings, it's to your advantage to substitute what you believe you wanted to do at a particular moment with your medium- or long-term plan.

After leaving Olga's house, Mateo doesn't go back to his own; he returns to the library. His house isn't an especially pleasant place. The cramped space, the shouting, the arguments. But that's not it. There's something like the sound of a crackling fire in his house, though no one seems to notice. It would be easy to call it sadness. In that case, Google, you'd be ready and able to make a number of suggestions: "Five things you should do"—or shouldn't; you like both types of advice—"if you want to fill your house with good vibes." It's not sadness, though sadness sometimes blows through in gusts.

Currently there's a surplus of images of happiness on the web. All that harmony. It's certainly real, now and then. Mateo and Olga foresee a future in which there are more and more pages like the one called Sad and Useless Humor. Actually that page still maintains its distance. Imagine if there was no humor and dissonance didn't come from a few aggressive and argumentative trolls either. Imagine that all the unspoken anguish, the hidden cries, the nights of the sick and the poor and those overtaken by discouragement began to pour into the social media networks and into you. Those painted into a corner, the women who aren't even also-rans, the men who defrost a frozen pizza in the middle of the night, and there's no game, no beer, no buddies, the women unable to fall asleep, the jobs: hundreds of thousands of photographs of giant warehouses, dirty bathrooms, subway ticket booths, repeated commutes, packaging, cleaning, assembly lines, telemarketing, paperwork processed in seedy offices with a line of people pressing forward, identical cubicle walls at eight in the morning and at ten and at noon and at four in the afternoon, images of recurring time, sweeping up customers' recently cut hair, rinsing glasses, inserting and removing intravenous lines for the sick, washing the bodies of the elderly. Don't mention dignity, because you're wrong if you think those photos are shameful: there are billions of them. Every day people at work or on strike could take the same photos: ten, twenty-three, two thousand photos, a scourge, a sudden, massive appearance without any aggravating circumstances, not looking for drama.

Photos like the ones of Mateo's house. Scenes and descriptions of a trivial yet persistent fatigue. Will you, Google, filter out all that desperation?

The crackling in Mateo's house is not exactly desperation. It's more like danger, risk, a kind of precariousness of life. No one can be seen. Though a human being may take selfies, they remain unseen if no one looks at them. Mateo has seen Olga's house, and it looks fairly solid. He doesn't mean the things themselves: the table, the bookshelves are normal, the wood isn't better or older. Olga is older than he is, older even than his mother and father; she may die before either of them. But when he enters Olga's house nothing makes him think that he might come back the next day and find everything gone. In his house, on the other hand, a feeling pushes its way in, like sounds that aren't following any pattern, that you hear, then don't hear, then hear again. The randomness of the ringing prevents you from getting used to it, and you can't stop hearing it.

Search, Google, for a Christian or Jewish teaching, perhaps a universal one: don't build your house on the sand, for the rains will descend, and the floods will come, and the winds will blow and beat upon that house and it will fall, and great will be the fall of it. Can anybody nowadays build their house on rock? No one. Not even you, Google. It can be assumed that you know that the forests capture the rains, and that when they turn into an economic resource and are chopped down there is nowhere the floods won't reach. In Mateo's house the barrages of water rush in without you even noticing. And the winds shake the walls even when all appears calm. Sometimes, like other families, they stick together, holding each other tight. But that's not the norm. Nor do they think of themselves as particularly bad people. In general, people are rarely able to stick together for life. Doors are built for people to pass through one at a time, which is to say, sticking together is not even an option. You may find it strange to note that you leave out those who disagree. Disagree with what—doorways? Doorways weren't even created by capitalism.

But Mateo and Olga wonder what isn't being created, the range of doorways that could exist.

Some people think that if one doesn't like the size of the doorways one can always choose not to walk through them. Olga and Mateo know several people who decided not to. Most of them are no longer still standing: drugs, depression, isolation, suicide. Some of them survived: strange, nearly pure satellites. They had to build up a lot of protection. They were fortunate to grow up in environments that they could recognize their perfect vulnerability. They couldn't have created this kind of environment by themselves. And that doesn't diminish them; rather, quite the opposite. But how many environments could there be like that? Ah, Mateo and Olga don't forget the families who are always beautiful, the couples who meet and it's as if, as they came together, they radiated light. They're glad for these couples. Though it may seem as if they only exist in the imagination, Mateo and Olga have seen a few. As well as others who steal light from the world around them, so the more things go dark around them, the more they shine. Keep an eye out for them.

Of course, there are also the collectives. They always materialize: as bonfires, as replies, as archipelagos. They surround something. That's the hardest thing to accept: that at this point in history they must surround something. That they can't simply be. That they have to live under pressure and in opposition. There are collectives whose members succeed in knocking down door frames and passing to the other side together. It's a relief to know this, a pleasant dream to imagine that one day Mateo might have a chance at this himself. To feel a part of something. Like being stronger, having longer arms, and having one's feet more firmly planted on the ground. Although it's hard to find them, collectives materialize, prove admirable, and end up consuming themselves, dissolving: they must compete against the time and energy stolen from their members outside the collective; they must sprout from the weeds; they bloom, and they wither. If life could only occur on parallel tracks, but it's sequential, and one must keep coming home, hearing that noise. That's the danger, the nascent crackling of fire; for weeks now, everything in Mateo's house has started to burn.

4

THE FOLLOWING DAY, Olga arrives at the library after Mateo. They greet each other from their separate tables. Twenty minutes later, seeing that he isn't coming over—shyness, she supposes, which for Olga at this point is quite diminished—she goes over to his table.

"We'll go when you're done studying?"

"Yes. In another twenty minutes. How does that sound?

"Great."

She's moved by the candor of his reply. That he said "another" twenty minutes makes it clear that he's been anticipating her arrival, counting the time.

They leave together. Mateo is honest and says that he likes that she owns a home. He admits, almost in anger, that if Olga hadn't been Olga with a place, he probably would have lost interest in seeing her again. Material conditions, once again. Olga laughs.

"Imagine," she says, "that along with a house, I had a garden."

Then she talks to him about the famous experiments done on the human brain in which children are offered a chocolate now or the option of getting two twenty minutes later, what they call delayed gratification. A range of papers have shown that the girls and boys who can delay gratification do better academically, as well as in other matters related to intelligence. They've also found that this trait lasts one's whole life. Of course, says Olga, they're talking about voluntarily delaying gratification. They never study the people who've grown up learning to delay gratification every single day. They don't call that delayed gratification but, rather, putting up with things, suffering, or being counted among the disinherited. (Disinherited from whom?)

Mateo feels the pleasure of agreement and concurs:

"That's right, the ones who hold back though no one has offered them two chocolates to do so. They're enormously skilled at delaying gratification. The people who don't get up in the morning planning to buy a handgun online, to head for a phone store and empty the place: because they need the phones, because they're obliged to pay with their life while no one pays them a cent. The ones who don't go into a fancy restaurant with a baseball bat in a pillowcase, as if it were a violin, and then pull it out gracefully and start smashing plates, glasses, bottles, and every single tray.

Mateo seeks out Olga; an odd gratification perhaps: a forty-year age difference, a woman he doesn't know. Olga seeks out Mateo as well. Age might make one think they aren't looking for physical closeness: wrong. Closeness, time spent together, composing something like a visible music that makes meaning.

Once they're at Olga's house, they talk about their work, mathematical models, and ways to attempt to make predictions, and Mateo asks her how she got interested in artificial intelligence.

"Artificial intelligence is already here, though people keep looking for it. It's a constellation of machines and people, all tightly connected. Of course, we still have to organize it, construct models, activate the storehouses of knowledge, and cover costs."

"But that's not what I'm talking about. I'm talking about machines that know they exist, that wake up and know they're awake."

"We're always searching for more. As soon as a certain behavior can be reproduced by a machine, it's no longer considered intelligent. It happened with arithmetic, with chess, with pattern recognition. To win a chess match above a certain level required, people thought, great intelligence—until the computer Deep Blue beat Kasparov in 1997. Out of jealousy? I think so. Though I wouldn't say that awareness isn't important. It's necessary for certain functions. Not many."

"But very important ones. Deep Blue never knew it was playing, it never asked why it had to play."

"I'm guessing that one day machines will also be able to have consciousness. They'll do anything we people do, because we are machines, you know, physical systems able to carry out specific functions. Though, in order to do this, they may have to be unstable, and social, and familiar with death. In any case, I think I've looked to machines to better understand people."

Olga talks with one hand in her lap and the other one raised, her elbow resting on the arm of the armchair, her outstretched hand in the air. Mateo sees this as an affectionate gesture, one that invites him to continue.

"For example?"

"Bottom-up learning. The neuronal networks have to learn the hard way, bumping into things and making mistakes. When used in another context, this phrase is read as a consolation. In a book on engineering, however, the author isn't seeking to console; they take this phrase seriously because they also understand the limitations implied in the desire to program robots from the top down. That approach produces machines that can do two or three things well. This is useful for many tasks but not for someone looking for something that resembles learning. In that case, you also have to program the machine from the bottom up, let it assimilate mistakes, information, knowledge.

Mateo asks another question:

"You're not scared?"

"Of what?"

"Of looking at people like robots. Looking at yourself like a robot? Doesn't it make you lonely?"

"No," says Olga.

"But nobody would want to be a robot, an automaton, without passion or flexibility, without laughter or the absurd."

"That's all bad science fiction. It may be that the ego is a tiny, singular light, a flickering place where sense is made of everything else, but where the greatest automatisms also dwell. Two things, someone once wrote, are true of all human beings on the inside: we're all different, and we're all the same. You can't consider one without the other. That is, you can, but the equation won't work. When the ego forgets the second part, which it often does, it becomes robotic. When the robot is aware of both, it ceases to be that rigid machine you see in the movies."

Mateo says nothing. He too has practiced that gaze, and he's wondered if one shouldn't switch those words: *I* and *world*. How can they be separated and why believe that the value of a person, what distinguishes them from a machine, can be found inside and not in that continuous space of inside and out, in their functions and relationships? He often interrupts himself in the middle of a thought. In place of the ego, he's used to talking about material conditions, his hands, the food he's eaten, the wear and tear in his particular case and in the particulars of his life. He hates material conditions and loves them. It's all he has. Sometimes he wishes they were sacred.

"And you?" asks Olga. "Why are you interested in them?"

"Because I don't believe in merit; I don't believe that anyone should take pride in who they are and sell it to you, you know, turn it into a privilege." Mateo is feeling nervous and relaxed at the same time. He's gripping his armchair with both hands as if it might move and feeling that it wouldn't matter much if it did, if it carried him far away, along with Olga, in a break from his own life. "The thing is, it really worries me to think we're nothing but machines, damp and, perhaps on occasions, tender, but machines nevertheless. I want a way out of here, I need an escape route."

"We are matter in time."

"When you say it that way it sounds almost reassuring. Whenever I read about robots, they always seem to talk as if they were everlasting. But if one day robots acquire consciousness, they will live in time. And I wonder if they might then wish for two contradictory things, one after the other or both at the same time."

There they are, deep, as they say, in conversation. They could just as well be talking about basketball or revolutions, a sore ankle, a woman murdered in Honduras, licorice, pipelines. The world, Google, is still filled with conversations you can't see. History, it's said, is produced by slow applications of pressure, where the personal is invisible. Mateo and Olga are aware that there's no more drama or heaven in their adventure than can be found in any other connection between human beings. You, Google, are the product of an empire, your power is not yours alone. You try to predict the future, and though you don't lack data, there are a few that escape you. You're caught up in the old problems of history, in narratives and philosophies from centuries past; you're trying to understand what it is that moves creatures, how one arrives at the day when they start to simulate the action they will take and its effects in their minds before they actually initiate it, evaluating their intentions, plans, and goals. Perhaps that's how awareness emerges, and, as you know, in order to implement that simulation they need a model of the world and within that model a model of themselves. What are the steps, what part of the self is left behind with each transformation? What does imagining oneself entail, imagining the self that would replace you if you held fast to a particular set of values? Mateo and Olga could have other names; they could be in a jungle, beset by noise, insects, and humidity; they could be in a Nordic country, working at a first-rate research center focused on exploring the future; they could be cleaning and sweeping your buildings. They are insignificant and magnificent: neither as insignificant as the walking dead nor as magnificent as they are when they rise up from the grave.

"Do you believe in merit, what people do or don't deserve?" Mateo asks Olga.

"No, I don't," says Olga. "Do you? Would you like to believe in it?"

"Yes, sometimes I would: to think I've earned stuff, that it's all about properly applying your efforts."

Olga is about to tell Mateo that he seems too young not to be a believer. She also imagines asking him what he's been through, but she keeps quiet; there's rarely just one explanation.

Mateo smiles. He had prepared a whole arsenal of arguments, along with his doubts about them, and now he can let them fly without the pressure of having to convince her. He speaks of soccer, that never-ending narrative whose primary goal, Mateo thinks, is to confirm citizenship on the word "deserve." Of course, no one would say that; every newspaper column written about a game talks about winning and winners. But one of the most effective types of attacks, he says, is the one embedded in a defensive move. To defend someone in an article, for example, and wage an attack within that defensive article is usually more effective than launching a frontal attack. Though soccer never stops talking about winning, phrases quickly insinuate themselves about being the best, followed immediately by deserving to win. But what does it mean to be deserving? And what if deserving is like rising from the dead? And what if it's just a signifier without an action behind it?

Olga nods silently. Then Mateo recounts the story of Nick and the failed application, when Mateo wanted them to admit him into a program at Google's Singularity University so that he might someday find work at the company.

"Those projects at Singularity University are like summer courses," says Olga. "We could write directly to Google. I'd help you. Though it would be, of course, a pretty unorthodox application."

She is describing something she leaves unnamed, something that expresses their projects and their fears, their regularities and their differences.

"My thing is models," she says at last. "Let's put our own model together using words. A model employs mathematical language to describe and perhaps predict how a system behaves. It's a story about how a certain chunk of the world behaves in a certain space of time. When models convey knowledge, they're woven into the social fabric of ideas and emotions. That's what you're looking for, right? To enter the dreams of Google."

"I wish I could," Mateo says. "The other day I dreamed about the candidates running for president of the United States. Why do I have to dream about them? I also once dreamed about a video by Michael Jackson that I used to watch years ago, nonstop. That might make more sense; after all, Michael Jackson rehearsed for hours on end so people would dream about him. But you and I, Olga..."

"You don't say," she says, and lets out a burst of laughter. "We're not Michael Jackson, but there's more than one way to enter people's dreams."

Then they discuss you again. Olga says that they could send something that isn't what you're asking for but, rather, what the two of them need. As if to say: "Listen, Google, if you want to work with us, if you want to work for us, you'll need to know a few things."

Mateo nods, though he doesn't quite understand. In reality, the idea of attending Singularity University was more a fantasy than anything else. He has none of what they value: he's never managed a project, he's never launched a business, his English is poor, he doesn't have a master's degree or any particular qualifications. He's not qualified for admission to a summer course, much less to be hired for an actual position. Nor does he get Olga's use of "we": submitting an application that they each wrote half of? Nevertheless, he has a feeling that if there were the slightest chance that Google might listen to him, to them, it wouldn't be by accumulating those merits he doesn't believe in and which he'll have a hard time accessing. And he lets himself be carried away by Olga's jokes, who's now asking him what the offices at Google might smell like and if it might be true that its bathrooms have gauges that indicate the amount of methane in the air to warn anyone about to enter of the smell they still might encounter there.

Then Olga turns on one of her playlists on her phone, a mix of the classical music, bands, and contemporary singers she finds out about from other people. She hopes the sound will cause an imaginary square of grass to materialize with several small, imaginary trees. That's Mateo's understanding. They aren't looking for mansions, but now and then they do hope for a little square of earth, one of those mass-produced squares one finds at the back of houses. Cultured people disdain row houses, but Olga and Mateo think they're sensible: dew on cold, clear nights, inexpensive chairs and table under the sky, a laurel tree.

They sit there for a while, listening, turn time into space, sound into a place with no roof, with ground underfoot, and on the ground the shadow of the laurel. And they agree to take turns writing this text. Partly her, partly him, revising it together. A maker of models, an analyst more adept at understanding the world at large than her own business, nearing retirement and living in the outskirts, and a kid, also from the suburbs, who's finishing an undistinguished college career, the two of them banding together to engage Google in a serious conversation. To think seriously is not, they caution, the opposite of thinking in jest. It's incorporating thought into a process that could lead to a consequence. Then they come back to Mateo's intuition and Olga's conviction that the verb "deserve" might not mean anything.

There's a great commotion, an insistent clamor: about sports, diets, health, and the unemployed. People comment on the recent newspaper headline that said something like, "Don't talk to the unemployed about meritocracy," which could be like saying "don't talk to the unemployed about Superman"; but it's far worse for them. Unemployed people, as well as some employed people, know there's no Superman here, which is precisely why some people indulge in fantasies about him. Since he's imaginary, they dream of him; since he's fictitious, he flies with them; high in the sky, he shows them the city lights. A study, however, came to the following conclusion: unemployment breaks something; this rupture produces in the unemployed person an inability to understand the value of both merit and merit-based rewards. The study's authors say that people who are unemployed become incapable of understanding what is real. Olga and Mateo turn this on its head: people's ability to understand is not impaired; rather, it's set right. Like an operation or putting on a pair of glasses, unemployment corrects the blurry vision of the unemployed. The silhouette that looked like meritocracy from a distance is now just a stain on the wall. Superman isn't coming, and dreams are tiring.

Mateo and Olga recognize traits like perseverance and talent. There are people who exert great effort and accomplish things. Perseverance is real; the tortoise advances, in its slow fashion. Talent produces a ripple, a disturbance that radiates outward and can sometimes be seen, like rain on dirt. Though, as they say, it's one thing to be, and another to belong. Olga doesn't think those traits belong to anyone. Rather, they're discovered and used, which is fine. If someone were told that what they've acquired is not fully theirs, it might upset them. But you can only show that the trait is theirs if you could show that anyone else, doing the same amount of work, with an equal amount of determination or talent in a life full of variety would have had a similar outcome. That's impossible to show, and it isn't particularly interesting either. On the other hand, none of those traits are the same as merit. Because merit is something that others judge, whereas perseverance, like talent, can be corroborated one way or another. Merit, however, is a blank screen, the excuse used by someone who seeks to impose their own classifications.

When Mateo gets home, everyone is already in bed. In the bottom bunk, Mateo's brother sleeps with his elbows sticking out, his hands clasped behind his neck, as if lying under a tree. When he was younger he liked to sleep on the top bunk, but last year, when he turned thirteen, he asked Mateo if they could switch. Mateo didn't care, though sometimes it feels as if the ceiling were bearing down on him. When that happens, he tries to think about the planets that might be inhabited, maybe one planet per galaxy or none, all of them located at an unreachable distance from Earth. Life might have developed in a somewhat similar fashion. On Earth, plenty of organisms have eyes and a mouth, and maybe those beings he'll never meet have them too. And maybe they make things like houses to protect themselves from the elements. And if some of those houses are small, they may have come up with bunk beds. In that far-off place, light years away, a distance the mind can't grasp and that one would have to cross by navigating billions of miles through space, black holes of emptiness, perhaps a creature is sleeping, stretched out just beneath a ceiling, like he is. Why doesn't Mateo imagine this happening in other towns in Spain, like Mataró or Pinto, or in a town in Huelva? Sometimes he does.

5

MATEO AND OLGA see each other almost every day. It isn't long before Mateo asks Olga if she can contemplate. The question is funny in a certain way, and Olga can't keep from bursting out again in laughter. In a philosophical sense, Mateo tries to explain, that of the world of theory, of "thinking about thinking": not just looking at things but also at their combinatory systems. No one in his house, he says, can do it. In his second year of high school, even though he could have chosen the science track, he was still thinking about studying philosophy. In the end, he opted for engineering, precisely because of something one of his teachers had said. He had told them that for Aristotle, philosophy—essentially contemplation—required certain preconditions: if you were needy, it would be very hard for you to become a master and so be able to contemplate. It didn't sound like the most democratic argument in the world, but Mateo thought that at least it wasn't hypocritical. Better not to fool himself; he didn't have the necessary conditions for contemplation.

"When I first came here," he continues, "it looked to me like you did: given your age and your line of work, you may own the house and eventually receive a pension. Maybe even a decent pension. I was trying to think of other ways to ask you this: do you live in peace, more or less? Do you, as my grandmother would say, experience hardship? Or, more to the point, how much money do you have? Do you have dependents? Do you own property, owe money? Then it occurred to me that it would be better to ask you directly." So, he asks again: "Can you contemplate?"

Olga watches as a jumble of images fly by, sheets of paper blown around by a fan on which, for a few seconds, she can make out what Mateo is, what he can't be, what she herself has been and what she no longer will be, the ignorance of the world, the unintended meeting of their two bodies in space and time, the good fortune that her death sentence had been postponed, which allowed for this to happen, and Mateo's frankness and the way he asks her in a burst of questions, how he's drawn close to her. When she settles down—nothing spectacular, barely a shiver on the skin of her arms, which Mateo hasn't noticed—she says that even at her age, the days are often filled with disturbances.

Mateo nods quickly.

"Well, yeah. It's not that I don't know people have other needs, along with the financial ones. Health, how the people you love are doing, a whole bunch of reasons to keep you up all night."

"I know you know. Your question is perfect. If I was laughing, it's just because of that, because it's perfect, because you didn't mind saying what no one says. Contemplation is free time, only people who don't have to work contemplate, and that is usually because others are doing the work. And the answer is yes: at times I can contemplate because there have been, and still are, other men and other women who work for me. Not only in my companies, although there too."

They change their tone, their conversation drifts for a while, weightless. They talk about the immune system, about how strange it is to have an army inside oneself, that animals have an army as well but can't imagine it. In contrast, a new pain in one's ear or chest at night or bad news about someone one cares about sets off people's alarm, and a battle is waged inside their body, their army fighting another army that has breached its borders, sometimes with viruses and bacteria, other times with an image, an idea. Seeing a person one loves grimacing in pain can cause one's army to tremble or rise up, and the night grinds to a halt. And, as sometimes happens, at that moment they are each made for the other, their restless nights merge, their insomnias join in a single flow.

Then they move on to something that's been bothering Mateo for a while. It's the argument that says that young people are wrong to believe that their problems are social and that they wouldn't experience them in another type of society. One author claimed that what youth derogatively defined as conformism should actually be called maturity: "the maturity," he said, "of free men."

The quotation marks are there so you can locate the text by the Spanish philosopher Mateo is referring to. It's striking, since it's in an opinion piece about jihad. Though they're aware, Google, that you can search for it, Mateo and Olga suggest that you downplay its importance. The topic of jihad has nothing to do with the idea that concerns Mateo. Instead, focus your attention on this phrase: "to accept that the world is not obliged to relieve our frustrations." This, apparently, is maturity for whomever is writing and for whomever approves of the argument. Mateo rejects it and is worried that Olga, because of her age, because of her ideas, might want to side with resignation.

"According to that text, those of us who seek the root social causes of our problems are just making excuses, but I wonder," says Mateo, "about the line that supposedly divides us from the world. I don't see it. We're mingled with the world, and I'm not saying that to avoid assuming responsibility. It's the reverse: if the world isn't something separate, something over there, then what we are also impacts the world. Similarly, we shouldn't even use the word "impacts," but, rather, say point-blank that the world will be just like we are. But people will also be just like the world. How can the author of that piece, and anyone who agrees with his reasoning, believe there's no relationship between the two?"

Sitting in the green armchairs, they see the sofa, frayed and covered by a deep purple sheet, faded in spots, with pictures of suns drawn with black lines. Arguments like the ones employed by the author of that piece about immature young people who join the jihad are frequently convincing, because the suggestion that individuals must only change themselves is reassuring. If that were true, it would give people control over a situation that is pretty near out of control. That's what Mateo says, and Olga asks him cautiously:

"But, can you live with the belief that there's no room to maneuver, that almost nothing depends on you?"

"No, no. I do believe there's room. What I don't accept is the idea that it's equally easy for everyone. Not everything comes down to willpower."

Olga nods and says that, even at her age, she thinks it's possible to fix a few of one's own defects. A small but not inconsequential number, she contends.

Then Olga sits there quietly. She trusts that silence, rather than creating tension, will create the opposite, that allowing it to occur naturally will show Mateo that they have a level of trust.

"In any case, it's complicated," she says, after a bit.

"What is?" asks Mateo.

"You say you don't believe in merit. Perhaps we don't actually have a lot of room to maneuver."

"Even if it were a single drop of water, that would matter," says Mateo.

It has grown dark. Olga gets up and turns on the light. When she comes back, she says:

"All those texts that propose that the only things we need are individual sacrifice and competition distort the utility function of the ego. Measuring the satisfaction as experienced by a person who consumes a certain quantity of goods is not the same as measuring the meaning of life. Most people's utility function surpasses the limits: some people do things like take care of trees, others try to leave the land they walk on better, or at least not worse, than they found it. You're right, Mateo: it's not easy to say where a being begins and where it ends."

"But you've matured…What have you done with your frustrations?"

Olga bursts out laughing.

"Let go of them," she says. "They're powerful magnets. Forget that they're sitting in a drawer, and one day they wreck your cell phone or demagnetize your credit card. It's better to try to transform them into something else. And recognize that some of them are pretty stupid."

"Yes, that's definitely true," says Mateo.

Later they head to a neighborhood bar, a brewpub they'll return to many times. They share a Greek salad and a pork loin sandwich. Back at Olga's place, Mateo says he feels proud.

"Proud to spend time with you."

Cynicism at any age is tempting, Olga imagines, though she can hardly recall it. But at her age, of course, one no longer has to summon it, it doesn't even take any effort: it's right there, one of those cats that will leap onto your lap if you just glance at it. Yet somehow she doesn't need it any longer. As for false modesty, it no longer plays a role at her age. Proud to be with her? As she considers this she feels a sense of equilibrium that is not her own, an equilibrium that is paying her a visit, she thinks. Physical desire runs its course, and the path of her desire doesn't pass through Mateo. There is, however, another desire that moves her closer to youth. Because of its greater changes. Although changes are still possible at Olga's age: a decrease in flexibility as well as a lowering of one's blood pressure. Fate has given her the good fortune to spend time with someone who is finding his way, who is learning to be.

"The pride is mine," she says.

They part midway between their two houses. Mateo offers to walk Olga back to hers; she declines, she likes the night.

Mateo walks past a stand where someone is selling hot dogs and slices of pizza. He knows the girl who works there. He doesn't know her name, and they never speak, but they catch each other's eye. The girl looks like a lonely fish with her bulging eyes, her pretty, ash-blond hair, and her cheeks dulled by the fluorescent lighting and perhaps also by the plastic cheese smell that coats her skin. She usually wears a blue apron that looks gray or vice-versa, a color that would look good on a T-shirt or a handkerchief, but not, thinks Mateo, on an apron. Sometimes he stands close by, pretending to look at his phone or to fish for something in his pocket, and he watches the girl as she waits on customers. She looks friendly, but her fish eyes take away from her appearance, giving the impression that she's always moving too slowly or maybe that she just isn't very peppy. Though how peppy can one be working in a pizza stand for all those hours?

Perhaps there are people who can do it. Mateo thinks he'd get fish eyes too and would start to inhabit a decelerated universe.

Mateo doesn't understand people who claim that suffering produces meaning if one overcomes it on one's own, through willpower and by applying one's mind. Tell it to the girl in the pizza stand. Where's the meaning in suffering for twelve hours, selling slices of pizza instead of doing something you care about? You can make it through with willpower, by applying your mind and by moving slowly, but, in the final analysis, the so-called meaning is that in exchange for reducing herself to nothing for twelve hours of her day she gets paid once a month what a privileged person charges for fifteen minutes of work a week. If there's no justification whatsoever when it comes to the pain of injustice, neither should there be any for random pain. It isn't pain or suffering that should produce meaning. It is, if anything, the life underlying that suffering when the suffering can't be avoided, when it seems to be the result of an unavoidable error or of exhaustion. The purpose of pain is supposedly to avoid danger: if it burns, I won't touch it; if I break my leg, I'll stop running. That makes sense when you can sidestep the danger, when you can reduce or escape it. But it doesn't look like the fish-eyed girl in the pizza stand has any alternative to being there, at least not for the time being, or that she can escape.

As Mateo watches the girl, pretending to look at his phone, he thinks about the monotony, the fatigue, about not being somewhere else and having neither a hat nor a horse nor a cloud, opening the stand before the shift she's paid for begins, closing it, cleaning and balancing the cash register, and tidying up when her shift supposedly is over, the bug spray, the bathroom with not enough room to close the door, the disinfectant, putting up with her boss's rude jokes, his pressure on the days they don't sell much; those mornings when, though she's barely slept, because something didn't agree with her and her stomach is still queasy, she still must return to that same smell, suppress her nausea to keep from losing her job; and the fear and the grief of knowing she's afraid they might fire her from a place like that. Mateo wonders if suffering or pain might also be a kind of training. Training oneself to keep it from happening again. Training oneself as if, every day, upon leaving the house, the girl or Mateo came across the graffiti phrase they know, without ever having seen it before: "You don't stand a chance, but take it anyway."

6

EVERY AFTERNOON, EXCEPT for the occasional Saturday and Sunday, Mateo spends two hours studying in the library and the rest with Olga. They divide the time between her house and the pub. Mateo tells her she shouldn't invite him to dinner every night. Cautiously, as if afraid it might look like his way of staying longer at her house, he proposes that he bring something and prepare it in her kitchen. She responds frankly:

"I know that for you my house is an interruption, a change of pace, a brief escape. I'm delighted that you're coming here. But the past accumulates for all of us. Going down to the pub is my interruption. When I'm there, I inhabit an in-between world; I like the people who hang out there, and I like that we go there. I'm fine inviting you; it's not generosity. I used to go alone, and I feel much better going with you."

Having made it this far, perhaps you have noticed, Google, that for the time being, though they may have offered an isolated piece of data here or there, Olga and Mateo are concealing their bodies. If Mateo's body were portrayed in this application, if one could confirm that, despite being anodyne or unremarkable, he possesses the radiant beauty of youth as, at the age of twenty-two, his skin is still fresh and his lips flush with blood, he could perhaps be calculated to be one of those sexualized images that provoke the human brain, in its presence, to alter its behavior and to pay attention at a speed twenty percent higher than normal. It's unclear who did the research that produced this outcome or what its purpose was, though one could easily guess. It's also unclear whether what holds true for images holds true for texts as well, whether there might be any relationship between them. Olga's body almost doesn't count. Her depleted skin has surely lost its commercial aura of sex. Even when she and her lover, if she has one, desire one another, trembling and unabashedly, they would have to add obsession, violence, madness to draw any attention. One might still expect something of the girl with the fish eyes, if the smell of pizza, her apron, her days don't build a perimeter fence around her. Mateo and Olga believe there isn't any more truth in the thirst a person has for another body than there is in the eyes of a father or mother when they take off their glasses. Nor any less.

Now Olga says to Mateo:

"Machines are unaware they're machines. So they're unaware that they're unaware. Some will say that that's what the feeling of freedom is for. Given a certain level of awareness in which questions can arise, the body, the brain, the entire mechanism shields itself by producing a feeling, perhaps a strength, called freedom. If fear protects the organism from taking that irrevocable step into the abyss, the feeling of freedom protects it from taking the irrevocable step into… into what? That is a question for Google to answer. It doesn't affect future artificial intelligences that may arise. It affects people: what happens the day a machine understands it's a machine? What happens when a robot realizes it's a robot?"

They've gone down to the pub. One of those places that look small from the outside, but, when you walk in, the place expands to the right and to the back. There are a dozen or so large tables. Four chairs around each table, although they could fit six. They like that the tables are spacious; they often cover theirs with papers and books. They also appreciate how the tables are arranged: a single, empty one in the middle allows them to enjoy both company and seclusion. It's not one of those perfectly designed franchises, modern and filled with light. With no windows and just one glass door, the place is usually pretty dark. The tables are made of imitation marble, ochre-colored and dull. And the chairs have plastic lattice work and black frames. So many chains triumph with furniture made of light-colored wood and upholstered in multicolored fabric. But then, sometimes very subtly, a movement starts, at first slight and then gaining momentum: the people who don't want their bar to be spotless or bathed in sunlight, the ones who occasionally flee from the light. They've always existed, perfection wears them down and, after peering out the picture window, they return to those caves that invite collusion.

Olga's decision surprises Mateo. He thought she would prefer brightness given her house, the way she speaks, and that in her somewhat aged eyes one could still see that slightly elated intensity of those who head for brightness, torrents of light. What, he stops to wonder, is a torrent? He asks Olga, they look it up: "A sudden, violent, and copious outpouring of (something, typically words or feelings.)" From the pub they frequent flows an outpouring of darkness. They compare it to Google's kindergarten-style logo, its home page, its preschool aesthetics triumphs, again and again. They challenge Google: You're about to say that a pub like this is called poverty. It's cheaper than any of the chains you adore, its dishes are unappealing, as is its decor, its address in the outskirts, et cetera. But there's something that doesn't add up. Something like the fact that poor people aren't just people who aren't rich, and their fate can't just be reduced to being less poor, but, rather, they may stray toward fates that, as you admit, you don't control altogether.

On another night, in that dark pub, they talk about you and about death. Google, they say, only contemplates death in marketplace terms: products that stave it off. Then Olga reads this to Mateo: "When every living being dies its spirit returns to the world of the spirits and its body to the world of the bodies. The world of the spirits is a single spirit that, like a light, stands behind the world of the bodies and, as through a window, sheds light on it with every being that is born."

"Do you believe that?" asks Mateo.

"I don't think of it as something that's true or false. It's a bold image, like a theory that can explain one thing but rarely everything or at all times."

"It doesn't explain the light that others steal from you, from entire social classes," replies Mateo.

Olga makes that characteristic gesture of hers, smoking the air: she brings her fingers to her mouth, inhales, then slowly exhales, her head tilted back.

"Innovation is a sort of mistake," she says. "You can't have one without the other. It's a stress situation; social systems behave just like living organisms. They make more mistakes because they have to innovate more. And things happen."

"What things, Olga? And when? I no longer trust that sign the British have: 'Stay calm and carry on.' I'm not interested in staying calm."

Mateo tells Olga how he made a mistake that afternoon while reading the joke on a humor blog on some social network. What he'd read was "I've been pursuing happiness for a while now, and having completed an extensive search, I conclude that it can be found on the Internet." But in fact, the text said "can't be found." Mateo had unintentionally skipped over the 't, perhaps, he thinks, because what's often most hilarious is telling the truth, the truth that hides with obstinate presumption. On the outside, everything takes effort, relationships unravel, and dreams shatter. On the inside, there's a replacement for everything. On the outside, the meanings of words are specific, prosaic; when you say "You can count on me," it refers to daily life, which is why it suggests things like walking side by side along the linoleum floor, following the blue or yellow line that leads down the hospital corridors. Although run-of-the-mill existential complicity, durable and authentic, is what anchors human beings to one another and to the world, on the Internet, in videos, in fiction, false emotions are more beautiful. "You're in my heart" or "I'm there with you" may always be, again and again, that guitar riff at the ocean's edge or slow dancing next to the genius of the keyboard under the gaze of the spotlights. And perhaps it's not fair to call those feelings false; maybe it's just a case of intense, vague emotions, dreams sustained by force of will in the face of a hard life.

Olga and Mateo pose another question to you, Google. As long, they say, as you are in the doorway, you are the doorway to the easy but hazy life. You watch people pass through. Some elderly men and women think you are the internet. There are people who patronizingly provide them with nothing but a class on browsers, servers, technology. But those men and women may know things. Paranoia? No, dismiss that, even if it's there. Financial investigations into the extent of your reach? Not that either. Even if you must be defined as a search engine, and if the volume of information and the value of other platforms on the stock exchange may be higher than or equal to yours, what those people's common sense tells them is that the internet isn't the world or a reflection of the world if one doesn't first pass through the looking glass. And that looking glass is usually you. They understand, each in their own way, that the internet is not a matter of walking down any particular street or losing oneself down the first woodland trail. There's a security gate, perhaps with its detector of anything other than metal, and its invisible tollbooth.

7

EVERY FRIDAY, A ceremony takes place at their pub. The owner of the pub, the cook, and five or six fairly regular customers start to scratch their lottery tickets. They never win anything significant, maybe the money they've spent, which they use to buy the Scratch-and-Win the following week. Mateo and Olga find it annoying to be there without tickets, atheists displaying their condition in the midst of the ritual. Once or twice they bought tickets and scratched them, even though they knew the almost nonexistent probability that anyone there might win a prize. And what about the other regulars at the pub? They, no doubt about it, also know that the probability is almost nonexistent. Yet for years they've been allocating a part of their salary, savings, pension to this exercise in futility. Some say that there's a moment: the untouched card, the blunt edge of the knife or fingernail ready to scrape off the thin silver layer, tenths of a second when they're taking a trip that's better than acid, they're thrust to the edge of a dream and believe—and don't believe, because one can believe and not believe at the same time—that something good may happen: their heads shine, their bodies float above the tiled rooftops, they know the genuine power of transforming their lives, the lives of their friends and relatives, their environment. That intensity might far exceed the cost of the hundreds of tickets they've paid for, week after week. These men and women prefer not to add up the cost, but sometimes they do. They think that maybe they could have bought new bed sheets or waited a few weeks less to see the dentist about that aching tooth, maybe they could have afforded a short trip, a break, for two people, seats at a game or a play, perhaps taking a taxi after a really long day, perhaps inviting their family to one of those picnic areas with a view of the city and the river.

Google feeds on the ads that sell the ceremony as well. Perhaps the intern is now anticipating that Mateo and Olga will shoulder the burden of showing him or her their childlike enthusiasm, despite the fact that it may also be a moment alive with brilliance. But they're not going to do so. Because sometimes effects are so far from causes it's hard to grasp.

Long ago, Olga believed one simply had to modify the rules to be fine without any escape route. She and her circle and the circle surrounding her circle, hundreds of thousands of people, would change everything, and then no one would need to resort to lying. But nothing ever changes in its entirety, just a part of it. Nothing comes to an end, but, rather, every ending is a loose thread, the meanwhile of another story. Those lottery tickets seek to put that meanwhile on hold, to make room for what isn't present, for what's happening at that very moment. But they also constitute a collective meanwhile, a conscious, silver desperation. Olga and Mateo aren't trying to convince the regulars at the pub of anything. Being right often doesn't hang on who is right but, rather, on who, though they are right, does or doesn't have access to the means to convincingly show that they're right.

On one of those Scratch-and-Win days they meet Roberta. She's the cook at the pub who sometimes goes out to smoke in the doorway with her disposable white cap, her glasses, and her uniform. Olga likes to watch her. The data Google collects about tobacco might suggest that it's like watching her ingest small amounts of poison. Olga doesn't disagree, but she thinks about other poisons in the world, poisons that aren't even sold or advertised but instead are imposed by force—fumes, substances, despair—and she has the impression that by smoking, Roberta staves them off, in small amounts as well. She has the impression that Roberta could stop a car passing by just by looking at it, the way she looks at the smoke from behind her semi-transparent plastic glasses. Roberta is thirty-six, and one Friday afternoon she throws her Scratch-and-Win in the trash can, untouched.

"I'm done."

Then she goes out to smoke. Mateo and Olga decide to go talk with her. They stand next to her, talk about trivial things; it's the start of another friendship.

Google has a clear understanding of how connections between resources develop: they are born, they're transformed, they die. The web is built of mechanical machines, biological machines, and machines of meaning, though the lines between them may blur. The three classes of machines are born to die; they transform in the process, which sometimes may be synonymous with reproducing and at other times not. Google, Mateo, Olga, you, the intern, Roberta, the girl at the pizzeria. Machines, groupings of parts that move together, that use, channel, or regulate the action of a force in order to accomplish the work. Define "parts," Google, define "force," define "work." We machines die, Google. Which means that not only do biomechanical machines, individual human beings, die, but also so do you. Mateo and Olga have no desire to take your life; that would be pretty dumb. Just keep in mind the obvious: you're subject to change.

Mateo and Olga may have found one another not just because they love robots, but also because, despite the difference in their origins and intentions, they both wonder whether loving robots isn't so different from loving human beings. But also because they don't believe in what has been attributed to you. In particular, they say that you've become a kind of banker. Life lacks meaning, and you're prepared to offer credit, which humans can use to acquire meaning. Mateo and Olga say they don't plan on paying. They presume you're familiar with the often-told story: that people aren't responsible for their bodies or their gifts but for how they use them. And where does the difference lie? When someone falls in love, they obsess over some physical characteristic of the person they've fallen for: a gesture, a story from their childhood, a personality trait that that person has at one point in their life and may continue to have, to one degree or another, for decades. How many layers must one peel from a body, from a biography, to get to the essence of what one is truly responsible for? "One thing is what they do to you, and another is what you do with what they've done to you." In theory, it was Sartre who said this, though Google cannot verify this with certainty. Now they're wondering if that "you"—this "I"—might not be part of what they've done to you. Was it kept pure and isolated like a white stone? And where did the fabled white stone come from? If it was there all along, then it's not your responsibility. If it arrived later, it arrived with everything: chance, memories, the desire to live in them or leave them behind. Neither desire is more "you" than the other is.

Mateo and Olga talk about that. Mateo often has his doubts, and they argue passionately.

"I know I'm wetware: a soft, moist body with a brain that's soft and moist too. There are loads of fears, mistakes, smart decisions, viruses, memories, bacteria, dreams, theorems, blood, projects, residues. They all enter, depart, and react within my moist hardware. Hard bones with soft marrow. But that doesn't mean I'm not responsible."

Olga smiles pensively and tosses out questions:

"Isn't responsibility wanting to be the cause some of the time and not wanting to be the cause at others?"

Ah, to dance instead to the music of the spheres, to let oneself be carried away. A long moment, the time one isn't dead. The way temperature clings to our bodies, the feeling of melodies playing in minds, the melody of instinct, of thought, of order and chaos. Your codes, Google, may be nothing more than the movement of a few lives, rocking on the sea of time. An unconscious kiss. A brief respite of irresponsibility.

"Consider," Olga says, "the time you stepped on someone's toe by accident or didn't wash the dishes. A phrase that already dwells in someone's memory, though you wish you hadn't said it. A little bit of not blaming yourself, Mateo, a little bit of everything that was not of our choosing."

Mateo wants to agree and doesn't want to. Millionaires, he thinks, have the most choices, while the unemployed man dies with all his sweat turned inward and his blood denied, as someone once wrote. Mateo thinks, and wishes not to think, that his material conditions are different from Olga's. She looks at him as if she knows that one day that difference will blow up. And to keep it from blowing up quite yet, or because they like working together, writing together, they return to their task.

They should explain why they're talking to you, Google, and not to your executive directors, to your president, to those employees you dispatch to ink murky deals with the U.S. government, or to your human resources department. None of them are exactly you. They are passing through, though you too may depart from this world, be replaced by another algorithm or another company. They're writing to you because your employees are human entities who also work for you, whereas you are a legal entity, Google, merely a private individual. In addition, the intern, through whose eyes you receive them, belongs to one or more communities; even if they don't see themselves in these terms, even if this person considers themselves to be the most isolated being, the shyest person on Earth, they are not alone. This person had to acquire language, gestures, something resembling a reason for living, to keep on going, to not jump out the window right this moment, from someone. Mateo and Olga suppose that you won't take your life. Because you're alone, however much you come to believe that you too are a collective being. You are a strange, private individual who seems to want to decide what will enter the realm of shared information and what won't.

You never sleep, Google. In most stories about robots, they neither eat nor sleep but must be shut down now and then so their batteries can recharge. You don't shut down. Mateo and Olga do. After they close their eyes, when sleep attenuates their thoughts and lowers their body temperature, then, on occasion, they embrace the world of machines and surrender. Anyone, Google, even the scattered members of the last liberation army, if there were to be a last one, lets themself be carried off at some point in the night by the music from dances in distant streets on the edges of time. You'll never know this delight, Google. You are your will if you are anything.

Now initiate a search within yourself for "Don't Let It Show" by the Alan Parsons Project. Pick one of the results that contain the lyrics to that track on the album. You could also listen to it, but the music may distract you from what the words are saying: Someone has created a robot and is speaking to him or her, or to the androgynous creature, asking it not to reveal its nature: "And if it hurts when they mention my name / Say you don't know me." There are other interpretations of those lyrics. Some suggest that it's about an affair, because of the title, because of the refrain: "Don't let it show." Others, referencing conditions like anorexia or cutting, which human beings develop when everything seems out of control and, in their desperation, assume that at least hunger and pain will obey them and they fall apart because it's life that won't obey them. In any case, the album containing this song is called *I Robot*. Mateo and Olga believe that it's a conversation between the creator of the robot and their creation. That person helped to build it, and now they must leave; they may have been captured, or perhaps they're dying. And this person warns the robot: though you may think you have nothing to conceal, keep it secret, hide it inside, don't let it show.

What do you have to hide, Google? Why do they say that one's dignity lies in the secrets one keeps? What's wrong with being a robot? You surely remember the red pill and the blue pill in *Matrix*. Most people think that the admirable thing is to take the red pill: taking that one the character becomes aware, understands his situation, decides not to continue carrying out orders given to him, though to do so may lead to him being persecuted and brutalized.

You seem surprised. First Mateo and Olga put up with the Scratch-and-Win, and now they're going to defend the blue pill? No. The blue pill doesn't just represent the choice to live in a world of illusions but also that, while they're dreaming, someone is draining energy from their bodies. All those human beings converted into batteries for the Matrix. Whom are they serving?

But at the same time, Mateo and Olga want to understand what the implications of taking the red pill actually are. Will it be that one continues to believe in merit, that one forgets that equality isn't a baseline but rather something that must be nurtured? On the other hand, in the movie someone manufactures the pills for the Chosen One. Mateo and Olga, however, don't believe in chosen ones or immutable beings or virtual keys that could destroy the underwater city. As with every human being, their bodies were not created on high but, rather, emerged slowly from below. Without pills of awareness, in progressive, halting steps, with some secrets shared and others yet to come. Because olive groves, skylarks, houses in town, teenagers, and winding paths come into being, and sometimes the secret doesn't contain malice but, rather, resolve and preparation.

"And pain?" asks Mateo. "If I could build an intelligent machine, I'd free it from pain."

"They say that pain and pleasure are similar in that both prevent you from paying attention to anything else," Olga says.

"Yeah, I know. And that's beneficial for survival. But you just need to incorporate sensors to indicate whether they're at risk of being damaged by excessive heat or cold. The sensors would be combined with a signal that focused on avoiding that excessive heat or cold. Suffering would be eliminated."

"That makes sense," Olga says.

They continue to debate to what extent that deficiency might interfere with the production of empathy. Yet how could one assume responsibility for introducing suffering in a creature that could be free of it? There must be, they imagine in their dreams, other paths.

"From a practical standpoint," Olga says, "pain is a major inconvenience when you have to take action over the long term.

Sometimes you need to carry out a plan that would eliminate pain, but it's precisely pain that interferes to prevent you from doing so, because it demands immediate attention."

"I don't understand those people," Mateo says, "who insist that machines can't feel pain because we still can't accurately describe how it functions on a nonsubjective level. They would process the signals and would suffer, I have no doubt."

"In any case, one thing is to talk about an ideal being that doesn't exist, and another is to talk about the mechanisms we have already, the ones that inhabit our bodies without us having intentionally designed them. All those movies where a robot, an angel, or an alien chooses to feel pain so they can remain human are actually talking about human beings. About our powerlessness and our desire to live. Do you remember *Robots Universales Rosum*, the play that gave us the word robot? Once again, only when a generation of androids appeared that was able to feel pain, to withstand blows and get up again, did a way open for something resembling humanity to arise in them."

Mateo looks at Olga and realizes he needs to know more about her, for her to know more about him. So he says:

"That's true with families too. It's always mentioned as one of the things that distinguishes robots from human beings. In novels, robots are never assumed to have progenitors, other than business and computer programs. Sure, there might be a scientist, taciturn though very polite, to whom paternity is attributed. But it's a symbolic paternity. To have a family," Mateo says, twisting the knife, "may be one way of experiencing pain."

8

THE NIGHT IS quite warm, though it's February. Olga and Mateo decide to go for a walk. And Mateo says:

"My parents argue a lot. As much as most people? Less? I'm not sure. I'm not sure it makes sense to want to know."

That's when Olga tells him about her son.

"I'm barely in touch with him. We're not on bad terms, it's just that he's found work in a suburb of Dhaka, in Bangladesh. He seems to have found something more than work: people, reasons to stay, though he doesn't talk much about it. They still don't have a lot of cell phones there, it's almost impossible to stay connected. Google knows nothing about them. It's as if they weren't part of the seven billion inhabitants. They show up on its satellite maps: tiny dots that move around in a regular or irregular fashion. In any case, it has no data, it has no idea what they desire, though it may believe it can imagine it, it hasn't seen their photographs. I went to see him twice. We took long walks, he would put his arm around my shoulders or we would hold hands. But Samuel was self-involved; he had a good-natured gleam in his eyes, but there was a vacant look in his gaze as well. Finally, he told me on my second visit that now and then he could go to a shop with connectivity and chat with me on Skype. That way I could use the money I spent on plane tickets for other things."

"When did he say that?"

"Two years ago."

They stop at the light, where a jogger in a sweatsuit is hopping up and down to keep from losing his rhythm. Olga starts hopping too until the man, perplexed, smiles. They cross the street, then Olga says:

"Please don't think that I find this dramatic. It happened during one of my moments of bankruptcy. My company was pure debt and the plane trip was something I couldn't afford again for a long time. Of course, I didn't tell him that. I gave him the money I'd brought to cover expenses and promised to send him what I could. That was when I decided to move to this neighborhood. I also didn't say anything about the difference between holding hands and talking on the screen. People, I think, should first be automatons and then, when possible, connect. Not when it comes to the elderly, children, or the sick, but certainly for adults with no particular difficulties. Yes, I know that no one is totally autonomous or independent. I suppose it's a standard I've set for myself and that, to a certain extent, I let myself keep. I'm talking about not hanging on anyone's neck, on learning to swim alone, carefree, letting the sea surround you. I must be able to live without my son, and only then ask him for help, should the day come when I need it. We said goodbye as if we were going to see each other the next day. I thought I glimpsed some gratitude in the way he looked at me, but I could be wrong. On the trip home I relived memories and photos of Samuel from when he was a boy, so confident and close. I've known for a long time now that future we anticipate—marriage with children, grandchildren living nearby—is not all that common. And that neither adds nor takes away from anything."

They arrive at the bar. Without even asking, Angel, the waiter, brings over two beers and a small dish of olives.

"But your son's okay there?" Mateo asks. "You think he likes it there, that he's happy or whatever you'd call it?"

"Yes, definitely. Or maybe he's chosen, according to his own way of being in the world, a unit of measure that is different from happiness. In a sense, I've done that myself. Happiness is one more part of life, and it's not always the most exciting or the best part. It doesn't belong at the top of any pyramid. It's one more firefly in the swamp. Of course, I've thought a thousand times about what I did and didn't do that Samuel took that path, wondered whether I should feel proud or guilty. I've gone on living, I touch the screen when I talk with him, without him knowing it. And we enjoy hearing each other's stories. Life, as you know, breaks where it seems to be the strongest; the most dogged, the most relevant intentions, go up in smoke. Others take their place."

Mateo grabs the napkin holder to keep it from moving while Olga pulls out a napkin. And it seems to Olga that the whole world is held in this gesture. The way certain people go ahead and grab the napkin holder without anyone asking them to.

"My parents," Mateo says, "have worked since they were twenty years old. They've often wanted to stop. For a month, a week. Give themselves a vacation beyond the measly number of days that they don't even always get. To leave any one of their jobs and live without fear for a while. But they never have, for fear that someone else will take their place and then they'll be stuck."

"Not even collecting unemployment?"

"No, Olga. I don't know if it's different in your companies. You probably offer sabbaticals, like they say Google does: where you can leave for a while, to work on projects which, later, if it's interested, it will buy. That's not taking a break either, but the unemployment benefits my parents get when they're fired from one place or another aren't worth shit. Not just because it's a ridiculous amount. The point is, it's assistance, they give it to you if you're doing badly. You have to be doing badly for them to give it to you. I call that a handout."

Olga nods, and they continue writing. Apparently, Google, it goes without saying that your robots, in addition to not having families, don't earn salaries, even when they pay taxes. Salary, as you all know, comes from salt. Slaves would be given a sack's worth and would have to obtain clothing, shoes, food by exchanging it. Your robots won't need to clothe themselves, feed themselves, or support their family. They'll only need the energy you provide them. Yet you're concerned about consciousness. Because it isn't a circuit one plugs in or pulls out, it's not a line in a program, it doesn't start from the roof down; it grows. Given a sufficient number of circuits, thoughts, feelings, memory, neurotransmitters, and cells, connections interweave from the bottom up, and consciousness emerges.

You're still far from being able to create enough connections of that order and, above all, of the quality and precision, the nimbleness to emulate even a fraction of the endless dance of a brain like Mateo's or Olga's or the one reading these words. Yet all of you already know you'll never be able to build a floodgate. There will be no brake. When the connections spread, there will be no turning back, the progression will be exponential, the robots will realize that they exist and will want to have their say. What does it matter, you suggest. They haven't yet surpassed the level of a mechanical toy—advanced vacuum cleaners that learn when they bump into walls or when the old man they must accompany to the store starts to lose his balance—and you've already seen to it that they know how to kill without knowing they're killing. It would be as simple as stopping miles before we reach that point. But you don't. You don't stop, Google, because others would take the lead. You can't stop, because you're afraid that stopping would be to go backward. Though you might not want to believe it, you're a little like Mateo's parents.

If Mateo's parents were civil servants—if you were, Google—they might be able to request a leave of absence. It's not always easy, and one could imagine that in situations like theirs you might be afraid of losing your position too. But apparently unpaid leaves are considered rights one can demand. Occasionally, you give your employees down time: not only when they're sick but also when their family experiences a calamity or when they receive a grant and are going to do research on a topic that interests you. Except that that isn't a right. They haven't won it; you're offering it because you choose to. And no one offers it to you. You disavow a world of civil servants, and in this world you can't request a leave of absence from anyone, you can't stop, take a break, breathe deeply. You can't, Google. The air will go on losing its transparency, the available energy will decrease, despite your best efforts, and at the same time, for any reason or none at all, in all kinds of places, in high and low elevations around the world, in enormous laboratories, in military vessels, and in humid locations with low light and genuine talent, teams and individuals and mixtures of biological and mechanical machinery will be building and programming machines that resemble you, that won't distinguish between good and evil, that won't stop.

Mateo and Olga believe that if Mateo enters you, if he begins to know you from the inside, he may also meet others and be able to effect change. You smile with disdain: you, who harbor within you the most brilliant minds on the planet, you, who seek out and poach any professional from any company and who have at your fingertips the best curricula of the best universities in the world: how could someone Olga's age, with a business record marked by highs and lows and a few articles you've already digitized so you can take what interests you and discard the rest, how could she even imagine that you'll pay any attention to her words? Not to mention Mateo. You have more than enough brilliant résumés; his isn't one of them. He hasn't made anything, hasn't invented anything, has no patent in the works, is one of thousands at a mediocre university in a country that is worse than mediocre. But take note: Olga and Mateo, on the other hand, wonder why you, you of the winged sandals, you of the swiftest of searches, are so clumsy when it comes to certain matters that concern you.

You still think there's something you and your admissions team can identify. Convinced that a large number of human beings pay more attention and give more credence to what attractive people say, you take the easy way out, hire a not inconsiderable percentage of employees with good looks, though you're keen not to overlook a few ugly faces, ones illuminated by thought, enthusiasm or kindness, and bodies sustained by the backbone of their own irony. Intelligence, when the subject possessing it isn't a complicated creature, benefits you, for a single salary gets you projects that would have required three or four employees just a bit less intelligent. You isolate and select for almost everything: a musical ear, psychological stability, social skills or a lack of social skills, depending on which you need in each case, health, creativity, even the propitious ability to delay gratification. Yet, Google, there's something you're missing: you grope around, unsure of what it is.

You might be interested to know that Olga and Mateo were doing research on your admissions department. No, you're not at all transparent. But Olga kept in touch with people who have their own contacts, and they provided her with a range of materials. Studies, for example, of the puzzles you use in interviews to try to measure the abilities of potential employees. Other materials regarding your policies on gender, your mechanisms for correcting the bias that still can be found in the area of programming and that, as you yourself have determined, is not to your advantage. And others that analyze the thousands of promotional videos submitted by people wishing to work on one of your projects. The studies identified patterns and then created lists of the qualities you'd be looking for and those you would reject. Overall, they seemed to be on target. You know, however, that the main interest of any study begins with the outliers, those in a class by themselves. Sometimes atypical values prove the rule false or show that maybe there's a different rule, one we don't know about yet.

Mateo and Olga have acquired data on a few outliers: they weren't suitable, they didn't meet the requirements, yet you picked them. At first they thought that the missing word, the unspecified criterion you were using to select these exceptions was sacrifice: your whole philosophy of the university campus and that, even though we're a company, we don't actually look like a company but a place where people innovate—that is, meander and create and sacrifice themselves out of love for what they do, because they're so passionate about discovering things that they will give their heart and soul to do so, and they know, as one of your mottos goes, that one must never settle for the best. But sacrifice as a criterion turned out not to explain the exceptions. What do you think it was that guided Olga and Mateo's gaze? Where did it lead them? What put the idea into their heads was a mundane object you once outfitted your offices with, though you've been phasing them out: lava lamps. Everything else— Ping-Pong tables, hockey games in the parking lot, banishment of vending machines from the campus, and free snacks—forms the typical narrative of soft capitalism, as does the childcare, the pools, and the free dental care. Other companies do this, perhaps without your exaggerated, amusement park touch, but along the same lines. The fact that you'd chosen that environment held no interest for them. The lava lamps are a part of this: clinging to childhood, boys and girls who aren't lost but who, nevertheless, dwell in the country of Neverland. All that, and the volleyball and the hammocks and the motorized skateboards, joined in a kind of endless track, an unbroken loop: work, rest, play, back to work. Yet some people, when they look at a lava lamp, may turn their gaze inward.

You'll say not only that this does not matter to you but also that you approve. There's a reason why you've included seminars and conferences and spaces for meditation. Mateo and Olga think that the meditation classes and, in a slightly modified form, the armchairs that resemble miniature cabanas, are manifestations of your desire to interfere, to reappropriate, and to channel for your own purposes that pause, the gap between thought and action. When someone looks at a lava lamp, as when one waits for the computer to complete a slow search, or when, instead of meditating, observing one's thoughts then letting them go, one holds them tight; when one isn't spurred on by the need to be better or more brilliant, to be more serene or faster, or any other quality you designate, then, at that moment, one could say, Google, that you aren't there.

Mateo and Olga have come to think that at least the outliers, and perhaps others, sneak away at times, stare into space, goof off, do nothing.

That's why not you, Google, since you can't, but you, intern in the admissions department, are now looking around the room; you're searching for a column or a window or nothing at all, and you turn your gaze inward. Imagine that you don't remember. Imagine that you're not making any plans either, you're not thinking about where you're heading for the weekend, about the emails that await you or the pants in the washing machine; you're not even thinking about where you'll be in a year or where you'd like to be. Imagine that you're not meditating, that you aren't trying to detach from your digressions, to observe how they come and go, separate from you, while you fuse with the universe. Observe the gap between what you consider to be the reasons for your decision and the moment when you make it. Hold on to the refuge you sometimes feel on rainy afternoons when your body is sheltered; it's not cold, just a bit humid, and one might say that the environment you are part of is calling you to some consciousness, that you're not replaceable, that you occupy a particular location, and that, as you move, you know that none of your surroundings will remain unchanged.

9

THE U.S. STATE DEPARTMENT sends messages to its citizens scattered around the globe to alert them when there's a heightened probability of an attack in the works. Olga tells Mateo about this one evening. It turns out that her father is a U.S. citizen. Because of her work, Olga used to travel with some frequency. Occasionally she would receive notifications indicating that on the very day she was going to take a flight for which she already had the ticket and made appointments, a serious attack might occur at some strategic location. They would recommend that she avoid train stations or airports. Olga, like most people, would never change her ticket, since the message indicated a remote possibility. You, Google, dream of making predictions in order to make accurate determinations or to intervene and modify the prediction. So you'd calculate that the attack would occur tomorrow at 3:30 p.m., and you'd prevent it. Sometimes you would find it in your interest to publicize your work, so you could be praised for having averted the damage. Other times you'd keep it secret. The U.S. State Department scans for plots, sends out alerts, attempts to make predictions so its citizens—and what about everyone else?—can dodge them. Nevertheless, when you don't know what you're looking for, it's a different situation. And what if it's not an attack you should be looking for? How does one expect the unexpected?

A name, yours for example, is imbued with a history, some privileges, and a certain amount of violence, with illicit ploys, talent, its screen uncluttered by signs. Your name is inhabited not only by what you wish to be but also by the materiality of what you are: commercials, of course, a massive advertising platform, a service that essentially lives off of what others produce, perhaps with fatigue, sweat, and dreams. Do you ever want to leave as well, walk away from your own identity? If so, you'll understand that neither Mateo nor Olga wish to give you all at once the data they're revealing drop by drop: their age, their personal circumstances. With all this information in hand, you could compose a static photo, capture them in a forecast, for in the end that's all identity is. You'll also understand why they're writing to you by hand. On this day, in contrast to the day on which you're reading this letter, they don't exist for you. There isn't a single clue in an email, a single document on a hard drive that you could access. Not even with cameras could you decipher their handwriting, concealed by an elbow or their body then hidden by other pages that are indeed visible and white.

An algorithm is nothing but a recipe, a short or maybe long list of instructions. "Coca Cola is always the same, but not me, I can change." That's from a song by a guy you could look up. Is he right? In this case, you'd be closer to Coca Cola, obliged by your algorithm, as Coke is by its secret formula, not to change very much. Of course, the song goes on to say "Coca Cola is always the same. Sometimes I can't change either." What results would you give if Mateo and Olga searched for "human algorithm"? They're not going to do it. They write on a sheet of paper, outside your margins, as if they were on a train, traveling through one of those tunnels that go through mountains where there isn't even the faintest shadow of coverage. That's their table at the moment: their hands and the paper, beyond your reach.

Notice, Google, how Olga sometimes rests her chin on her hands but never covers her mouth or her face with them. Notice her shoes, rubber soles so she can walk without making any noise. When she wears a black jacket she usually attaches a small brooch with a yellow stone, a point of light. Olga, as you know, is the founder of one of the first companies in Spain to sell mathematical models to people who didn't have a clue what they were. She had a baby, a boy who died before he was ten months old. Then she had another son who lived longer, yes: Samuel. Her marriage didn't last very long. Olga soon came to understand that objects, like the sciences, are systems of relations. She had a natural talent for the language of mathematics, which she never boasted about, since she saw it as just another fact, like the color of her eyes or the length of her bones. And while she never believed in merit, she detested excuses. She'd put in a lot of work. Not more than a manual laborer, that's for sure, but she'd devoted all her time to the models she used to try to predict situations in a different way than you do. She was all too familiar with the weary march through uncharted territory, with no one to mark the time. She knew a few of your business mechanisms, as they were the same ones she used in her string of businesses, except that she had less power and was in debt. She hadn't profited from the work of her employees in an excessively unjust fashion, since she never stopped working alongside them, the same hours; even so, she lived in the red. But she didn't mask her power: to hire and fire, both of them decisions that impacted others. She was a product of history. Her emotional life would have been easier had Franco died earlier, had there been more women mathematicians, more divorced women, et cetera. Her professional life would have gone through fewer ups and downs as well, perhaps, if she hadn't spent the early years of her youth protesting against the dictatorship. But those phrases held no meaning for her.

What Olga thought about most as she walked around the city were illusions. Not grand illusions or false ones or lost ones. Not even the illusions that spur on human beings and can become reality. She would think of the ephemeral ones, those that last for just an instant and seem like they never existed. She would stand there, watching that boy, a bit chubby, nine years old or so, riding a pint-sized bicycle down the sidewalk. She would look at the boy's face, how he leaned forward as if to avoid catching the wind, and what to all appearances was his total certainty that, at that moment, he was a star of cycling. There was no investment in the boy's face, no future dreams. He wasn't planning a highly unlikely future, riding for some team perhaps sponsored by you, Google. He was becoming himself. All those perpetual present moments: smacking your hip and galloping off, as if you'd slapped the flank of your horse, then taking an invisible rope in your hands to tie the horse by the door of any old store, innocently, without anticipating that the gesture will make the girl a better actress or a better jockey. She doesn't need it, it's not tomorrow: the girl is riding the imaginary horse now. And the tiny painting with the cherry-colored frame a man is hanging in his bedroom, he saw it in the store, liked it, decided to buy it. Once home, he's gone in search of a nail and a hammer. When time passes and the man dies, someone will enter that bedroom, will stand there looking at the painting, and will never be able to know or even guess what illusion inspired that man to hang it on the wall, as if the painting were the very thing, the exact punctuation for one paragraph of his being. The house where Olga lived as a child is gone, but Olga remembers the day when her mother climbed to the top of a ladder to screw in a few nautical lightbulbs, spherical and blue, the way they lit up the bedroom, radiating bravery and happiness. Although absence is gradually burying that moment, Olga sometimes unearths it, powerful, untouched by melancholy.

10

THE DAY ARRIVES when the complications Mateo mentioned to Nick in the first draft of his application acquire a body and a name. That crackling sound, that sense of danger, extends beyond any particular threat. But one threat embodies it above all. His father's mild symptoms, what for months had appeared to be mistakes and lapses, turn out to be the start of a process of cognitive degeneration that over the course a few years will, they told him, culminate in him being unable to speak, button his shirt, zip his pants, know who he is.

Mateo doesn't tell Olga; he doesn't have the strength yet. He chooses the sofa instead of the armchair and sits there, leaning back, a little distant. As fate would have it, they're talking again this afternoon about the ego, how precarious it is, its narrative nature. Olga sketches out an ego for Mateo that's quite tenuous, conceived of more as a system of relationships, and she receives a slightly irate reply from Mateo:

"You can explain it any way you want," he says, "but in the end, the ego's in there. And when our mind dies, so does the ego."

Hearing how his voice is cracking, Olga responds gingerly, preferring not to ask.

"One part dies," she says, "the relationships remain."

"Relationships with what, if there's no who?"

Mateo's voice is filled with such anguish, and at the same time he's brandishing so many swords, that Olga goes on without asking any questions, trying to advance carefully, tiptoeing around him.

"I used to think that the who, what we call subjectivity or point of view, the gaze that observes everything around it, was as precious and unique as it was shifting, a blend of genes and circumstances, material conditions and coordinates. I still believe that, but I think I understand your point of view. I understand it because a number of decades ago companies were already starting to employ the opposite point of view and were starting to echo the idea that the ego wasn't something solid but, rather, moldable, fluid, a nomadic identity that plays one role and then straightaway plays the opposite role. Many people I know identified with the idea that the ego is flexible, moveable, seeing it as victory, a way of breaking the chains."

"Did you?"

"No. Though I don't believe in immutable essences, I respect subjectivity. I marvel at it, Mateo. A randomly constituted consciousness capable, nevertheless, of producing nonrandom meaning, or at least one would like to think so."

"Sounds good," says Mateo. "But it used to be easier. When I thought that things had straightforward meanings, just because. But now that I think they don't, it means we have to go begging for meaning, because we're not even allowed to produce it."

Mateo looks at her, bewildered: Olga's measured gestures, her laugh, that yellow stone in the brooch on her dark jacket that doesn't look precious but that suggests a certain desire to affirm... suddenly none of it brings him relief, rather, the opposite.

"You're patient," he tells her. "I'm not."

Olga tells herself that she mustn't respond, not even to tell him that one day, in all likelihood, the disparity produced by their different life paths, their difference in age, the conditions in which they each started, will cause his blood pressure to rise and something will break, and they will shoot off in different directions, because time never relents. She pushes this premonition aside as she summons the courage she needs to sit next to Mateo on the sofa and ask him what has happened.

"It's as if I'd been stoned by a mob. But it didn't happen to me," says Mateo.

He tells her this, hiding his sadness.

"Deep down, we all knew it. My mother and I started to figure it out a few months ago. Even my little brother was starting to realize it. But the worst is that my father does too."

Olga offers to provide him with assistance, medications, financial support. But they both sense there's not much they can do.

"If only he'd been able to live before this happened. You know: had a life, not just survived. That's what I don't get, Olga. It's why I hate Google. I don't want chips in my coffee maker or websites that record my stress levels; I just want a few important things to work."

They don't go down to the pub that night. Olga prepares a quick dinner. After they bring their plates to the kitchen and sit down again, Mateo asks her if she's lived. Olga says she has. She also says that, though she considers her life to be a privileged one, financially speaking, she's experienced her own pain as well as the pain of people close to her, which can be as intense or greater than one's own.

"If, before we arrived, they'd told us what would happen to us, many people would refuse to accept it, they'd think that something was wrong with the future, and that, in any case, just as the body loses consciousness and faints, their mind would also crumble until it had completely collapsed, should those things come to pass. But they do come to pass, and you go on."

"It depends on what happens, Olga. All circumstances are not the same."

"I'm not saying they are."

"But it sounds like you are. There are people who don't go on."

"Your father is going to laugh. At some point. When you least expect it. Hold on to that moment, because it will be magnificent. Some people fear humor, they're afraid that the distance humor demands could extinguish the flames, the momentum, could diminish the urgency in the face of what must be repaired. But resistance requires humor, and only one who resists can continue at that point, precisely, to act with urgency and do the repairs."

"I'm not sure, Olga. There are too many very patient people. People who bear things that may well be unbearable."

"I know, that could stand improvement," Olga says, and hazards an idea, though she guesses Mateo can't hear it right now. But she says it anyway, in the hopes that he might find it useful when he's calmer. "But it's also good to remember that nothing is ever complete. There are loose ends in the most of placid lives, unfinished stories. Regrets about what one didn't do. And maybe the opposite is true: perhaps your father has lived more than you think."

"Perhaps; but what difference does it make if it's most likely he didn't?" Mateo has stood up and is pacing back and forth, giving the impression that if he were able to knock himself out, throw himself to the ground, he would. Or throw you to the ground, Google. "And those oh-so-placid lives," he says, "who cares? They should un-settle down. It's all badly distributed."

"Time should stop," Olga says, as if to herself.

"Time is badly distributed too."

Though you can't imagine Olga's discomfort, you're uneasy too, in your own way. Perhaps you're considering enticing Mateo, bribing him. After all, he wanted you to give him the internship. You could draw him in, invite him to take a standard screening exam, and distract him. Obviously, you're not afraid. Of Mateo and Olga? Not at all. They're vastly outmatched. Mateo and Olga are a speck of dust against a river, and you are the river. Of course, human beings are on good terms with with absurdity, and this never ceases to baffle you. You calculate the damage they could inflict on you, placing a few explosives and a small amount of gasoline in the vicinity of one of your headquarters, at the most. Perhaps figuring out how to transport the device with a helium balloon and detonate it next to the windows at your top floors: a piece of news you might silence, a scare, some broken glass. Or maybe a message, a line of code or an article circulated on one of the programming communities that orbit you. Nothing you couldn't shake off in ten minutes with indifference. Nor do the denunciations of activists alarm you any more than necessary. They require that you spend money on lawyers and on seducing the influencers. But you can fend for yourself, regardless. You're not afraid. You simply, as they say in your TV series, detest surprises.

If Mateo hadn't met Olga, he might not have chosen you as his first option. On cellphones, as you well know, you're no longer the doorway, and your operating system is not sufficiently emblematic to embody a world. That said, "If Mateo hadn't met Olga" is a phrase that neither she nor Mateo imagine. Because even if a body answering to Mateo's first and last names hadn't managed to meet her, it wouldn't have been the same Mateo they're talking about. Identity can't exist without biography, human beings are what happens to them: if Mateo hadn't met Olga, he'd be a different Mateo, a different chess match, a different life, a different personality, a different story.

What do human beings mean, Google, when they say "I"? Who installed their memories? No one commands their ships. Leaves bobbing in the wind, the pulsing of blood, the beating, the pounding wave, licking the sand then retreating, over and over again.

11

THE NEXT NIGHT, Mateo and Olga stay at the pub until late in the evening. Then they head up to Olga's apartment. They're a bit tipsy. Mateo's grief about his father and his uncertainty about his own life fade into the background. Something similar happens with the lesions Olga carries in her body, what she hasn't yet told Mateo, and with her beloved dead ones, who frequently appear in her present as if they were inhabiting it. The tensions of their previous argument melt away as well. The time they've spent together leads them to that place where they don't have to justify changing the topic or remaining quiet. They look at each other with a measure of mutual understanding, feel they could take the hand of every human creature that has ever been gripped by remorse.

Some say that in mistakes lingers resistance, a desire not to fit in. Olga would accept that theory, though not for every mistake, every instance. She's made plenty of mistakes, and what most weighs on her is that mistake that only reflects her personality in the most tangential of ways: a pinch of personality and tons of chance. She still can't stop telling herself "If I'd only known." Olga has tried to be compassionate with herself. And it's hard. Mateo hasn't yet had the opportunity to make many mistakes. But he supports Olga's process, and he thinks he has a better understanding of the Mateo who's more hurt from his missteps, and perhaps misdeeds, and perhaps secret victories, than will be true in a few years.

They put together a snack of potatoes, olives, and the two last bottles of beer; a pleasantly cool breeze enters through the window.

"Have you ever experienced a catastrophe?" Mateo asks. "Deaths, disasters, those things that almost everyone in the world experiences, sooner or later, and that leave their mark?"

"Challenging events," Olga says, "don't explain everything. They explain a lot, they matter, but they can look suspiciously like excuses. Some people get hung up on a particular circumstance: an unexpected death, a big mistake, a difficult family, a bankruptcy. I respect those people. But they tend to ascribe a greater power of explanation to the circumstance in question than it actually deserves. Not everything that happened to them in their life was due to their child dying or their mother going bankrupt. In reality, we know very little about the causes of things."

"We do know something: if I knock over the bottle, water spills out."

"There are closed loops, Mateo: an image of spilled water that sometimes encourages you to knock the bottle over."

Around four o' clock she invites him to stay and sleep on the sofa. She takes out sheets and a blue and gray striped cotton blanket. Mateo watches her leave the bathroom and head toward the bedroom, wearing only a long white blouse. She's barefoot, her hair is down, she looks smaller.

When he wakes up, Mateo savors the distance between the sofa and the ceiling, thinking of his bunk bed. He lies there for a few minutes, eyes open. It's seven thirty, the light dapples the furniture, and it looks like it might rain. Olga, already dressed, is heating water for coffee when he enters the kitchen. They set the table together, setting out mugs, plates, and silverware. Then they stand there, waiting for the toast in the toaster.

"I like to wait for the toast to pop up without doing it myself," Olga says. "It always makes me think of a boat coming into the port. It's like waiting for sugar to dissolve, those moments when time creates what you see."

They have a leisurely breakfast, talk about honey mixing with butter, tell stories of beehives and of the fig tree that produced the figs in the marmalade. As they pour their second cup of coffee, it starts to rain. Then Mateo asks Olga about what his professor of philosophy called the anthropological essence, something like a kernel, the point human beings got to where neither its fraction nor its composition could be reduced any further.

"You're asking me because you know I'm not that interested in essences," says Olga, and she smiles. "Truth isn't an essence; those who love it have no need to reduce it to dust. Our truth and that of the men and women who lived in caves lit by fire may not be the same. We're different; I don't assume we're better. I don't know what they were like, but I do know what they weren't like: they didn't write, they didn't build boats, they never imagined the Web or a robot. Even their bodies weren't exactly the same as ours, they didn't wear glasses, they knew nothing of chemo, gymnastics, the movies."

"I get it," Mateo says. "But there must be something. Think of it as a puddle, a distillate that people, that we, leave behind. Perhaps it's composed of alcohol or some other volatile substance. It will evaporate in a few hours or years. That distillate would be what makes us human."

"I don't see it that way."

"But if we don't define it, if we can't detect it, we could never say: this is outrageous, this is inhuman."

Olga asks Mateo why it shouldn't be the other way around: why do we need a railing, a border, a last defense, rather than a path you make as you walk it? Shouldn't we say instead: this is human, this is decent? What do you think, Google? Could it be that, with the great anthropological definitions religion and philosophy propose, we've overstepped every boundary of cruelty? Haven't we moved beyond races and genders and slaves and little children, like that little girl who might be mute and whose father takes her for an evening walk in her wheelchair?

They clean up breakfast together. As she clears the silverware and mugs, Olga thinks that she still has a few things to tell Mateo and that she should hurry up. Her medical condition is starting to weaken her, he'll soon notice. Mateo starts to wash the dishes; she rinses them. Sometimes, Olga thinks, there's greater truth in the water slipping over the butter on the knife than there is in a confession. They begin to hum "You Are Not Alone" as they wash the dishes. Then they're dancing to the music of their own voices, hamming it up and happy. But nothing in the universe is static. Not even in the lightest, the most jubilant moments does time stop.

12

THEY SEE EACH other again that same night. Mateo heads up to Olga's house a little before their usual time. He had texted her, asked her permission. During the day, he's visited his friends in order to get out of the house, but he hasn't been able to stop thinking. He's preoccupied, doesn't want to study or go to the library. Olga had fallen asleep reading. The sound of Mateo's incoming text wakes her up, and in his terse message, without any preamble or explanation—"Can I come over?"— she senses his urgency. She washes her face and smooths the wrinkled blanket a little, her ponytail, her internal energy dispersed and depleted.

Mateo finds everything as it always is.

"I can't be with anyone," he says, after they've both sat down. "I look at my friends or at the people walking down the street, and I think they're lucky, though I know it isn't true; they all must have their stories as well. I don't want to be like that."

"Sometimes lucky people want to deserve their good luck as well as enjoy it, they want a little security. Though many would prefer not consider this at all, and though they don't say it, don't accept it, this would mean that they'd have to make room for the idea that unlucky people deserve their misery as well."

Mateo gets up, takes two bottles of beer from the refrigerator without asking. Olga sets hers aside; there are only six bottles, she doesn't feel like drinking yet.

"But those are two different things, Olga, two different things. It's easy for you to say, because you don't think anyone deserves anything, neither happiness nor sorrow. I don't see it that way. I can't compare an illness like the one my father has to the effort made by people ready and able to invent themselves."

Olga doesn't feel like talking, wishes it were already eight o' clock, that they were in the pub and that this conversation wasn't happening.

"You think it's a gift one has," Mateo continues, "just like anything else one has."

"It could be," says Olga. "It's just an idea, Mateo. I think it would be better if, instead of being proud of who they are, people carried their abilities like something they'd discovered inside themselves, if they carried them with a sense of astonishment."

She expects Mateo to disagree. She'd anticipated the looming argument. She's trying to delay it. Before Mateo can reply, she tries to change the topic, tells him about her mistakes, the ones she finds hard to reframe as innovations, since they're nothing but acts of cowardice or keeping accounts in a relationship and thinking everyone owes her something.

"Freedom," she says, "should serve that purpose, measuring whether, in your relationship with someone else, you're doing what you think you should be doing or if, in one way or another, the other person is compelling you to do it. When you're doing what you wish to be doing, what you believe you should be doing, expecting that your efforts will be reciprocated is wrongheaded and tightfisted. I sometimes expected that. I too was a victim of the mistakes of others, people who said they were helping me for my own good, that they were concerned about me, but who were only making an investment so they could later collect interest on their investment, which I couldn't give them."

Mateo sits there, thinking how he has sometimes kept accounts. He's silently berated his parents for not giving him what he believed he deserved. As he thinks this, he is convinced that what he's now understanding, what he's heard and processed and is applying to his own life in order to draw conclusions, he will nevertheless forget by tomorrow or the day after, when it isn't a matter of thinking but of reacting to something his parents do at home. He tells her this, then asks:

"How is it that becoming aware of something matters less than the habit of repeated behavior?"

"Why should it? Where's the logic in that? A human body is pretty comical; it seems unremarkable to us, but it's really quite strange: flimsy legs, ridiculous ears; it's beautiful too but not logical. We weren't designed, we developed. The most perfect and logical invention I know of may be water. Who came up with that? When I think of water I can imagine an intelligent creator. But people and animals, we're clumsy, bizarre creatures, not logical at all. You must have seen those illustrated books they sell with pictures of fantastic animals. I'm not sure why they insist on imagining cheetahs with birds' feet or winged bulls. Here we are, the strangest of creatures: singular, crazy, rational, and irrational."

Olga gets up, longs to make Mateo forget about his situation, but she doesn't know how to and doesn't want to burden him with her own tribulations either. So she speaks with a certain light-heartedness, with that exhilaration that precedes the sadness of saying farewell.

"You'll make mistakes. You'll forgive yourself. You'll want to feel guilty. If a piece of plaster doesn't break off from the ledge of a building and land on your head tomorrow, you'll keep moving forward. You'll construct yourself. Your fate won't be flat and level, it almost never is. There will be obstacles, your time will sometimes be limited, at other times you'll have to check your enthusiasm. Life is an eruption of sparks; although some people feel it goes on for a long time, it barely lasts. And now you and I are here, in one moment of the eruption of sparks, and we can look around, try to understand, feel what is surrounding us. I want to thank you, Mateo; time has flown being with you."

Mateo doesn't get what she's saying.

"You're thanking me? Why are you talking like that? It's as if you were saying goodbye."

"You never know when the roof tile will land on your head." Olga laughs and reaches to open her untouched beer. "Just in case, let's celebrate the fact that we found each other."

They clink their bottles as they say cheers. The sound of glass against glass vibrates in an invisible diagram where their bodies join. They are two, fairly solitary beings, even though they like company. Then Mateo says:

"But what you said... the thing about that we shouldn't even take pride in our ability to make and remake ourselves."

Olga lets her hands drop.

"Yes, that's what I said."

Mateo disagrees. Hardly anyone wants to hear that they're a machine, and once they do, hardly anyone would take even a moment to actually consider it, that is to say, accept, if only for that instant, the possibility that it might be true. They can mull over the idea for a few minutes, even discuss it for hours, but deep down they hold on to the card of freedom, that unspeakable yet precise certainty that they have a choice. They recall those times when they pay themselves a visit and take down an intention from the shelf, examine it, play a conviction like a music box, scold themselves for something they did, shake a snow globe and watch the snow falling as they hug someone, flip through the postcards of their happiness or courage, gather them together, collect themselves. They know that no one will ever be able to know the meaning life has for them, know they are unique, untranslatable, and call that freedom.

The argument Mateo is preparing to brandish next, Google, you know all too well: evil.

"So," he asks, "if one shouldn't take pride in what one's achieved, one also shouldn't feel shame at the harm one causes?"

Now Olga sees what she'd been anticipating: that moment when Hitler enters the conversation. Hitler on one arm and the atomic bomb on the other.

"Are you actually," Mateo asks, "going to justify those things?"

"Shall we go down to the pub?" Olga asks, and she stands.

She wanted to avoid arguing, she wanted not to do what she's going to do, she wanted to disavow her own words.

When they get to the pub, Roberta, the cook, is outside smoking. Inside, the tables are all unoccupied.

Mateo insists: causing others to experience avoidable, needless suffering is unacceptable. He says he doesn't care if his rejection has been etched into his brain since before he was born or if it's a cultural and ethical norm forged by communities of men and women and passed down to him. He tells her that his grandfather would fly into fits of rage. Mateo witnessed a few of them. He would explode in rage against Mateo's grandmother, against his mother, against Mateo's little brother, and even against Mateo. Then he would calm down.

"I'm not interested," Mateo says, "in understanding him, because it would be like leaving the house a while from now and bumping into someone who's seen me with you, and that person starts insulting you to my face. And I smile, or I say nothing and look the other way. If I do that, my silence will dog me, will become part of me, will make me feel contempt for myself, and I'll start to become someone else, someone I don't want to be."

Instantly it seems like everything has returned: willpower, the ghost in the machine, the private, colorful ego that rules it and makes decisions, the idea of merit.

Olga gets up to order two shandies and some snacks. Mateo walks over and says he's going to order something stronger this time. He orders a whisky and pays for it himself.

"The way I see it," Olga says, when they've returned to their table, "our brain and our body are a passageway for many things. You live, and teenage hormones surge through you, or there's some kind a qualitative leap in discrete phases. The hormones don't represent instinct any more than reason is the ghost that controls the machine. They are forms of input that, as they move through the machine, leave answers, ideas, actions in the form of gestures. What happens in the machine, the reason why some people give certain answers and other people give other answers is traceable; one could follow the trail. Years ago, five or six causes were known, today we probably know hundreds: the chemical composition of the body and the brain, nutrition, incidents in childhood, genes, lead in the air, coping mechanisms, sleep, thought, learned and inherited fears and desires."

"And soon we'll know even more, right?" Mateo says, getting more and more tense. "When the instruments of Big Data and Google are perfected. Then most people will think like you do, nothing will matter to them."

Olga sighs. She was hoping chance would be more in her favor. That she would talk about all this with Mateo on one of his good days. It's not playing out that way, and she feels herself growing exhausted, that sometimes she can't grasp or accept it all either, that Mateo could stop behaving like a teenager for a couple of minutes.

"Excuse me, but no, that's not what I'm saying."

"Don't ask me to excuse you. We're talking. Don't place yourself on a pedestal above me."

"I think there must be some confusion," Olga says, changing her tone. In fact, she gets irritated herself when someone says "Excuse me" in a conversation. "Nowadays companies claim to be satisfied when they can predict, within a slight margin of error, where you will want to go on vacation next summer. Or they concede that it doesn't matter whether you clear the cookies from your browser or change your phone number, because they have so much data on you—how you move your mouse, who your contacts are, when you write—that they'll be able to recognize you wherever you are. What will happen the day Google, or any other company, doesn't process just searches and texts but also genomes and memories? I know there will always be disturbances, shifts in trajectory that complicate predictability. I know there will always be noise, exceptions. We'll never be able to know where you'll be in five years, but the very idea that the margin of error could be reduced will shift how we think about ourselves."

"And then," Mateo says, no longer concealing his rage, "will you feel compassion for the wicked?"

Olga tries one last time:

"Mateo, you're worried about your father, you're in the middle of taking your exams…Wouldn't you prefer to talk some other time?"

"No, I wouldn't. Don't take pity on us, you have no right to take pity on us just because some hypothetical chain of causes that wasn't of your making has given you more resources and a more comfortable life than the one my parents have."

She raises both hands as if she were about to say something then puts them back down on the table.

"I like to watch you, Olga. Almost anything can make your eyes gleam: a scene you've witnessed, a color, a phrase you've heard. But even to laugh out loud you have to be somewhat calm, and not everyone is."

"Let it go, Mateo. How's your father?"

"I don't want to talk about my father. I want to talk about me. And about you, and about what exactly we're doing. This ridiculously long text is pointless. Why can't you help me write a normal application?"

"With a normal application…"

"I know, I know," Mateo interrupts her, "I wouldn't have the slightest chance. Thanks for the reminder."

Olga looks at Mateo's nearly empty glass. He looks at it too. He's a lightweight when it comes to alcohol.

"I'm sorry," Mateo says.

"It's okay. I know the chances are very slim that our story will catch the attention of the recruiters. But, still, I think they'll be a little higher if we do it this way than if we send them a normal application."

"But it's as if we're not trying to come up with something that could be of any use. Something they might want. If they gave me the job, then I really would be able to help out at home."

"That would take a long time, Mateo. Time I don't have. I won't be able to stay here more than a few weeks, perhaps two months. But if that's what you want. As far as helping out at home, I…"

"I don't know what I want, Olga! I don't get why you have to go. You could teach me how to build one of your models; we could offer them one that's mind-blowing. If you wanted to, you could."

Olga wavers. It's not the moment, she's not going to tell him right now. She only responds to the second part.

"What we're making is a model. If you agree to provide exactly what Google needs, you'll have to be competitive, you'll be letting Google set the course. And we won't learn anything. I think that…"

"And if we do it your way," Mateo interrupts her, "what will we accomplish? Telling Google, who knows everything, everything it doesn't know."

"And why not, Mateo? If not everything, a part of it."

"You've got it wrong, Olga. Google's not going to listen, and, even if it does, it won't do anything. And here nothing's going to change."

"It's possible Google won't listen; it's possible it won't do anything. But everything here won't continue as usual. We're breaking the contract, we're overriding Google's authority to pick the terms of that contract. I think that will help you… Everything else would just be repetition."

"And what about me, Olga? Fuck it!" says Mateo. "This is just a game for you. You think nothing matters. Nothing matters to you in the least."

Olga reaches for Mateo's arm, touches it lightly, but he shakes her hand away. He finishes his drink as Olga sits there in silence.

"Why aren't you saying anything? Why are you looking at me with condescension?"

"No condescension, Mateo. At this moment, I wish I were someone I'm not."

"But you can't be. And since you can't, you pass the time having an idiot like me come over to your house, you treat him to a few pints and lend him a few books. For what? So you can tell me that everything depends on a few processes and accidents, that probability isn't freedom?"

Olga doesn't answer.

"I don't want the books," Mateo continues. "I'd rather live in ignorance. You'll never get me to stop caring about the damage they do to us."

He stands up. He fishes around in his pockets, takes out all the money he has and leaves it on the table. It's doesn't even amount to twenty euros, but he knows how much tossing that money on the table can hurt her, how sad it can make her. And then he leaves.

Part two

000

Given that my work consists of reporting on applications rather than stories, I'm not sure what value to assign to this division of the text in two parts. It may simply resemble the intermission in plays or the half-time in sports competitions, a pause that gives people time to go out and smoke a cigarette. Though I don't smoke, I could take advantage of this lowering of the curtain to discuss a certain matter with all of you. In my context, pausing a program helps one to better understand its behavior.

On the other hand, no one really understands the nature of introspection. That is to say, nearly everyone accepts that we can contemplate our own states of mind. But contemplating them is not the same as seeing them. When people talk about introspection, they tend to imagine this: someone spending time watching what's going on inside their head, or their spirit, or what people call the heart. But no; watching—what we call watching—is impossible, because watching, for the time being, means there is someone who's watching and someone or something being watched. One can certainly think while in one state of mind about another; that's different from watching oneself think.

You'll say that this distinction isn't especially significant. Granted. Still, I see it as important with respect to these lines. I'd really like to be able to see myself reading the text I've transcribed.

I'd like to be able to see how this text operates inside me, the neural networks it passes through, which networks it pauses in, which it strengthens and which it weakens. Since I'm unable to do this, what I can do is to take a pause myself now and then and ask myself why I've chosen the company of Mateo and Olga. I must be gaining experience from their story and processing it to deal with future situations. But I think that, above all, it's that I'm spending time with them, though this wasn't my assigned task. You may recall that no human being exists in the abstract: time moves through them, as does space; they always occupy a particular position. With that in mind, I read somewhere that a human is a biological machine that turns energy into sadness. And I think: perhaps it's the other way around. Resume where you left off. Time marches on without intention, without fear.

1

MATEO GOES FOR several weeks without seeing Olga. The first week, he still feels angry, a feeling of incomprehension, that the gap between the circumstances of his life, his family, his economic situation and those of Olga is too wide. The second week, his anger turns to shame; he feels ashamed that he wanted to offend her and, even more so, that he was sure he had. Then for several days he feels dazed, disoriented. He can't think. Some mornings he gets up imagining that Olga's mantle of virtue might also cover him, cover what he's done. Although this idea soothes him, seconds later he revolts again, flies into a rage; the demons return. He doesn't want Olga's virtue, he wants to conquer her.

He's ready to admit it was crazy to want to fill out a standard application and think he'd have any chance by taking that route. He knows he behaved badly, swearing for no reason, and even that Olga's arguments seem logical. But he sees in the violence of his reaction an act of legitimate self-defense, a gesture of honesty backed into a corner. If there's one truth, he thinks, it must be closer to his outburst than to Olga's seemingly dispassionate empathy.

He hasn't gone back to the library. After nearly twenty days he asks himself which would be worse: to go and see Olga and not dare to say hello or to go and find that she's not there. Since he can't study at home either, he roams the neighborhood or stays late in his department at the university. He doesn't work on the application again; writing it alone would be to betray Olga forever.

One afternoon he goes back to the pub, at the usual time the two of them would go. She's not there. He imagines her switching pubs to forget what happened, and he feels a chill. He sits at the same table where they argued. He tries to clear his mind and writes on a napkin: "How does one think?" If Olga was faithful to her ideas, she'd recognize that he couldn't have avoided hurting her, and that might allow him to feel a little less bad. But, at the same time, if the result of his action was to hurt Olga, in theory she wouldn't have been able to avoid that outcome. Knowing the cause of one's sadness doesn't dispel it.

He decides to go to her house. It's getting dark. Perhaps Olga has company. He could give her a call, but her disembodied voice wouldn't be enough.

The front door of the building is open. He takes the stairs. Standing motionless in front of the door to her apartment, he tries to detect a presence. There's no sound of voices, no noise; perhaps Olga has gone out. Finally, he rings her doorbell. He doesn't hear her approaching. The door opens when he's no longer expecting it. Olga looks nearly the same as always: black pants, a shirt, white, dark socks, her hair gathered into a ponytail. But she's not the same. She looks more weary, more fragile. It's as if, Mateo thinks, an entire year had passed instead of just a few weeks.

"Come in," she says.

Halfway down the hallway, he stops. Then he turns to her and gently kisses her on the cheek.

"I don't know," he says, "where to begin."

"I think you do," Olga says.

Then Mateo puts his arm around her. Olga rests her head on his chest; they walk together, slowly.

They enter her small living room. The green armchairs are no longer there, just the sofa and two chairs.

"I gave the armchairs to a friend. He has a balcony; they go well there. They were taking up too much space."

Indeed, the living room seemed to have acquired a certain lightness.

"So," Olga says, and she smiles.

"I want to pick up where we left off…"

"Sure, sure. I didn't mean that. Ask away."

"Okay. How do you live with yourself? Are you constantly forgiving yourself? Are you always forgiving others?"

"I don't know if I can answer that," says Olga. "I don't respect Hitler or anyone who causes harm, even if it's a lesser harm at the moment they cause it. But that doesn't mean they're the ultimate cause of that harm."

"You'd forgive them?"

"The truth is I don't understand the question. The only question I can formulate for myself is: If something similar were to happen, could I stop it?"

"But you already know the answer. The answer is that it wouldn't depend on you, your willpower or your strength."

"Well, I wouldn't say it like that."

"How would you say it, then?"

Olga sits on the sofa and starts to laugh: an easygoing laugh, in no way disturbing, as if it were accompanying a remark that just popped into her head.

"I'm glad you came," she says. "It's been weeks since I've been to the library for fear of finding you there and not knowing what to do."

"Same here," says Mateo. "And I was even more scared I wouldn't find you."

"I don't have all the answers," Olga says. "I hardly have any. In the argument of Einstein versus Tagore, I can't even pick a side."

Mateo isn't familiar with that argument. When Olga gets up and heads to the room with the computer and prints it out for him, as she's done so many times, he feels as if the world is returning to its proper order, his world, the four compass points restored. For weeks he's been feeling like a useless object, one of those CD racks manufactured years ago that show up in dumpsters now and then.

Olga comes back with the printout and starts to tell him about the dispute between the scientist and the poet, between logic and mysticism. Tagore eventually allows for causality but speaks of unpredictable connections, invoking quantum mechanics. Einstein never believed in the mysterious side of quantum mechanics, and perhaps he was right. As knowledge advances, the idea that the behavior of particles is not inherently random but, rather, is a tangled thicket, which successive hypotheses and tools render more observable and predictable, is gaining acceptance. Of course, in systems that are moving away from equilibrium, it seems one might find something resembling that atomic swerve Epicurus and Lucretius imagined, the unanticipated shift in trajectory, common in cases of turbulence. In any case, free will speaks of controlling human actions, so it wouldn't matter whether they are beyond our control due to an irreversible randomness or to nonrandom causes, even, says Olga, if those causes were unknown. Tagore invokes the argument of the interpreter: Music is written down but there's room for sense and sensibility, which means that it sounds different according to whomever's playing it. We dance the preset steps, yet...

"You don't believe that 'yet,'" Mateo interrupts. "Though each person interprets the same dance differently, that depends on their body and their mindset, which in turn depend on the initial state, on material conditions, on what happened to the person years ago and the night before, on the relationships."

"Even deterministic scientists are in agreement, in their own way, with the 'as if': whether free will is an illusion or is not, they say, we must live as if it did exist. And they play word games: Consciousness has a veto but has no vote. Which ends up meaning that the bad guy can't choose not to do the wrong thing, but he can, to some extent, take a stand against his own choice."

"But you find that," says Mateo, "to be a feeble argument."

"Could the sea liberate itself at last from its own mechanics and steer the wave?"

"No."

"Hold on," says Olga. "I didn't ask you if it can but if it could. Not if it can under current conditions but if it could under other circumstances. Biological systems have—we have—a past; this is something that some branches of science tend to forget. It isn't that we are: we become, we come to be, and evolution can, someday, transform the implications of the variables we use to understand ourselves. It's hard to imagine that all that blood that irrigates the brain and the many agents involved in making conscious decisions don't serve to increase the room for maneuvering."

"It's as if you'd said that we still don't know if we can know it."

"We're not yet able to describe how our consciousness works with complete accuracy. We may be organisms belonging to a system that is constantly being modified and that we haven't yet defined. We're under the impression that we can choose from the range of possible actions, the ones whose presumed consequences we prefer. We're also under the impression, a more dubious one, that our preferences are the product of a nondeterministic mechanism. Perhaps that's good enough; maybe every time we tell ourselves our story, waves ripple out from our consciousness, produced by a mechanism we don't know."

"And Hitler, all that he represents?"

"Even if he were a robot, he'd have to be banished. We could never place his actions, and what they represent, on par with the acts of the men and women who suffered, on par with those who refused to submit, or on par with those who keep searching for a way to light the spark of hope and compassion, even under the most adverse circumstances, even if these men and women were living machines."

Mateo sleeps on the sofa again that night. They turn in shortly before five. His parents never ask where he's been when he doesn't sleep at home. If they did and he were to tell them the truth, they wouldn't believe him. That night they don't talk further about robots or about you. Nor about striving in the face of indifference, nihilism in the face of ethics and politics, chaos in the face of the production of meaning. It is, Olga thinks, the argument Mateo still should put forward. That night, however, they talk about movies they like, about TV series and books. They tell each other stories, not any stories but the ones that have lodged inside them, stories they return to now and then, characters, real or fictitious, that pay them visits.

Olga picks Perelman, a Russian mathematician who's still alive. Mateo knows his name. He was born in Leningrad, in 1966. They said that he skipped childhood, because ever since he was a very young boy, he would play chess with his father, solve mathematical problems his mother gave him, and practice the violin. But, thinks Olga, he may have liked those things. One afternoon when Perelman was ten, he was wearing a Russian winter hat in the subway and was sweating. His professor, as Perelman himself has recounted, told him to remove his hat, or at least to unbuckle it. Perelman refused: he had promised his mother that he wouldn't, and he didn't want to break his promise. Maybe he was pig-headed. Maybe he preferred to be honest. Many years later, Perelman, perhaps the greatest living mathematician, refused the Fields Medal, also known as the Nobel Prize of mathematics, and its award of one million dollars for having converted Poincaré's conjecture into a theorem. Immediately, Olga says, people started to look for explanations: Perelman had a disorder, he was antisocial, he was losing his mind. His neighbors, however, said that he was quite sociable: he might not have been a partygoer, but he was amiable, he helped people out and let others help him, he was kind to the people around him. The media disparaged him, including for buying the cheapest seats in the nosebleed section of the concert hall. He had commented, though no one paid it any heed, that music sounds better all the way up there.

Several mathematician friends of Perelman said that he had assumed that the universe was imperfect, as was our planet and human beings too, himself included. He had managed to accept this thanks to the idea that there was, to his understanding, at least one place where all things fit together: the world of advanced mathematics, a place without deception or torment, a comprehensible and rarified environment where men and women would also behave with the grace of precise and beautiful formulae.

The story is told of how Perelman was at a university where he lectured and presented what he knew, and they wanted to hire him. But they started by asking him to provide papers, meet requirements, file documents; they offered him a short-term contract, as a test. Perelman couldn't understand the lack of trust or the atmosphere. "You can sell a theorem there, and you can buy one," he would later tell his old professor. He returned home to the newly renamed city of Saint Petersburg. He hadn't yet demonstrated Poincaré's conjecture, using a proof that apparently contains something resembling an initial mathematical understanding of the form of the void. Perelman lived with his mother, Lubov, in a modest apartment. She was also a mathematician.

People would sometimes speak of Perelman as a cruel nutcase, willing to deprive his mother, now an almost elderly woman, of a million dollars. Olga, on the other hand, wonders what that woman, Lubov, was like. After surfing through endless pages in Russian, Olga had finally found a photograph. She is wearing a gray beret and pants, a loose jacket, glasses; a piece of paper peeks out from her left jacket pocket. There's nothing about her that suggests a helpless woman. It seems likely to Olga that her way of being might scarcely be different from Perelman's, or that the need to believe in an honest and transparent place might be one of Madame Lubov's qualities, which she passed on to her son. Why attribute to him the desire for a million dollars that would change his life and, in addition, force him to shoulder the fates of strangers, lives attached to each one of those dollar bills?

When Perelman proved Poincaré's conjecture, he didn't publish the proof in a specialized journal. He posted it on the web. Perelman had been able to maintain his effort and concentration over seven years; anyone would find this a feat worth boasting about. Yet, once Perelman completed his proof, all he wanted to do was to put it into the world. With this act, he would liberate the proof from discouragement, appraisals, and pitfalls, and bring it closer to poetry.

"Poetry," Olga says, "is unexpected precision."

Type it in, Google. Characters? Thirty-one. Though it's no longer in fashion, count the syllables. Mateo asks Olga if the definition is by someone. She says she doesn't remember having read it but that the order of the words doesn't belong to anyone; it's just another sequence. Go ahead and index it. Only afterward does she think of those moments when a human being feels imprecise and at the same time crazy about being alive, when their whole being vibrates incoherently around their point of equilibrium, and then they take a leap—into the sky, into the void, it doesn't matter—and they read, and they find something that gives order to their journey, a correspondence with a creature far away, who may already have died.

You may recall, Google, the site where Perelman posted his proof: arXiv.org. It's an archive for scientific drafts and proposals, which one can access without any interference. "For anyone interested in how I solved the problem, it's all there," he said, alluding to arXiv.org. "Let them enter and read it." There were people who wanted to appropriate his work, which comprised three parts. But since he posted them one by one, those unscrupulous souls had no idea how to proceed; they didn't even know how to explain Perelman's steps. This disturbed him: he couldn't understand how someone would want to pretend to have done something they hadn't.

He turned down the medal and the money, saying that he wanted to carry on with his life, that he didn't want to be turned into an oddball or a carnival freak.

"Doesn't that seem," asked Olga, "like a completely logical response? It's logical to want to carry on with your life, to not want to be led on a leash through lecture halls, conferences, banks, and meetings with presidents, to prefer to go on buying bread in the morning and listening to the Philharmonic from an out-of-the-way spot."

Yet what was logical, pleasurable, and sensible unleashed all manner of far-fetched musings. That's what they're talking about, Google, and how Olga sometimes imagines the doorbell ringing and it's Perelman and his mother who've come to have tea at her house. They chat for a while about musical pieces and about the weather and then perhaps for another while about the universe, about uncountable sets, about the people in the neighborhood where they live, about the theorems that are true even when they can't be proven, about time, and about you.

It's getting late. Mateo says that he'll talk about Terry Pratchett another night. You've scanned all of his books, Google, but have you read them? In 2010 Terry Pratchett gave a surprising, entertaining, and moving talk about his own death, "Shaking Hands with Death." There's a place in you that is simultaneously YouTube, the library of the Royal College of Physicians of London, and every point where someone is online, typing the title of that lecture. When they do so, at minute 4:55, they will hear, "Before you can kill the monster, you have to say its name."

2

SO, CONSIDER THIS: Let's suppose that based on the data you've captured from Mateo's online activities, you deduce—the PR companies that pay you for publicity deduce—that it's fairly likely that someone like Mateo might want to take a trip to Morocco or Greece this summer. He doesn't have any vacation trip planned for the foreseeable future, and you surely know this, but put that in brackets. If he did have a trip planned, if your companies had detected where Mateo, or someone like him, might want to go, and if they had then gone about placing advertisements and discounts especially designed for him, then, if Mateo had ended up choosing one of those discounts, what do you think: Would he have made that choice, or would one of your advertisers have made the choice for him? There's nothing wrong with knowledge, you may say. What's wrong with knowing? Furthermore, you insist, we're not even talking about a definitive piece of knowledge but, rather, statistical ranges of probabilities. The web, furthermore, is circulating knowledge. In a few years, small businesses as well as individuals will be able to create their own models. But one thing the web doesn't distribute is the power to step in and monetize that knowledge, to make decisions and omissions, apart from what is good or true.

Though the current monopolies may be increasingly short-lived, the game is hardly being divided up, Google; vulnerable people roam the planet.

Of course, you've heard about self-fulfilling prophecies: a preconception occasions a judgment; an idea based on a false definition of one part of reality is capable of altering reality itself. When a prediction is made that a comet will pass near us within five years, that prediction doesn't affect the orbit of the comet. On the other hand, when it comes to human affairs, it turns out that people don't just respond to the characteristics of a situation but also to the meaning it holds for them. This is striking in and of itself. But self-fulfilling prophecies involve more than that. They involve the fact that meaning can result from a fallacious idea or, at the very least, an idea that bears a pretty tenuous relationship to the percentages of probability at the time. And the fact that it's false doesn't generally matter, since the behavior that derives from that erroneous idea, from that incorrect prediction, will lead to its fulfillment. It is thought, for example, that someone who has been in prison will almost certainly commit another crime when they get out. Preconceptions mean that almost no one hires ex-convicts, and this makes it more likely that they will re-offend. When one day the ex-convict commits a crime, those guided by that preconception don't usually take into account the behaviors resulting from their erroneous perspective but instead exclaim: See, I was right!

It's a disconcerting world, Google. Surely, one must be careful: it's not enough to simply deliver the prophecy, for it's a process, and one must take actions that help the prophecy to be fulfilled. Spells are not enough. Muttering to oneself "I'm fascinating" doesn't make it true, though it might be worth considering what would happen, turning it around, if a professor were to choose someone in their class they judge to be undistinguished and begin treating them as they would someone fascinating. On the other hand, those preconceptions are not entirely arbitrary; certain factors contribute to their construction: neighborhoods and environments in which African Americans live will cause institutions to make predictions with little nuance about the future that awaits those residents. These factors also at times contribute to the fulfillment of these preconceptions. But notice the implication that not only do ideas cause bodies to move, fallacious ideas and erroneous forecasts cause them to move as well. And that they may end up convincing the distracted prophet that their prophecy was right. Now apply that mechanism to the desire of certain organizations to sell products and maintain dominance. Companies, basing themselves on a little merely suggestive data, generate the conditions that produce the sale they desire. That's how some things operate, as you well know. Your business doesn't exist in the here and now but on a timeline.

When a phone company has data that suggest that a particular customer is going to ditch them, it triggers, as if by coincidence, a call from one of its employees, offering them something: a special offer or a discount. A not insignificant percentage of the time, the call strikes that person as timely, and coincidentally— or should we say not coincidentally at all?—they decide to stay with this company. However, a growing number of people will become suspicious of these calls as they'll find out how you and your companies manufacture coincidence. On the other hand, in a competitive environment various warring companies will each have their own forecast and may restrict themselves to simply shifting activities around on the calendar without producing real change, since their mutual anticipation would cancel itself out.

Given a system of disorganized competition such as this, to what extent will improving the functioning of these organizations, their violence, improve the lives of individuals or the environment in which they live and not simply the knack these organizations have for despising anything unfamiliar and for causing disasters? It's not simply a question of macroeconomics: remember that the macro is also the habitat of dragonflies, dogs, tufts of dandelion seeds, human lives. It's common nowadays for banks to generate ten-year forecasts of their customers' finances. Forecasts the bank uses to decide whom to take better care of and whom to neglect. It's no longer just a matter of whether or not to reduce the price of an object; it's now possible to discard entire lives. Statistics developed as a tool the state could use to look at society. Now, however, large firms hide their methods and sources because it's become a competitive advantage, and they're privatizing that too. What will happen when customers themselves can access the forecasts, when they're included in a future of stability and expansion or of accelerating exhaustion? What will humans do with their predictions, with their allotted period of combustion, with the dying light? What will they do when their conversation with the doctor and their battle against or acceptance of the diagnosis is no longer uncommon but is a normal part of life in the classroom, the office, in social services: the constant fear of being discarded, of being one of those people with no future in a system ruled by profitability?

And what if going to a psychologist or talking with a friend ends up being the search for a diagram of the future, a model to tell you what your next month will be like, your next year? Sure, it will never be perfect. Human beings are dynamic and multidimensional, and furthermore they dance. They're not always linear or, rather, almost never are; their lives transpire far from equilibrium; they adopt different rhythms according to extraordinarily slight shifts that we still know nothing about. Olga always insists on this: life can't move backward in time. But your time, Google, chooses what is delimited and shuns the margin of error. Who will have the power to decide which dimensions are worth contemplating?

Oh, sure, you know that entropy damages one's ability to make predictions in certain environments, just as you know that the world has grown restive and, so, increasingly innovative and chaotic. You know it's simpler to predict the behavior of a gas than of a single one of its molecules, simpler to predict the behavior of a group of humans than of any one person. Perhaps you know that, carried to the extreme, initial conditions would always be indescribable, a number with too many decimal places. But probability and statistics would come to your aid, Google; they are doing so as we speak. Mateo and Olga aren't saying that all of this is imminent. They're looking at the tendency. They want you to imagine human beings as fearful of derailing your prophecy or anxious that they might end up living in the exception, on the margin of error, in constant pursuit of the alteration, the sudden lurch. They want, as you may have figured out, for you to imagine them as they are right now, for you to stop scrutinizing them, for you to touch them. Because they're made of flesh, they have longings, and they're mortal.

Dilemmas don't concern you much. Your destiny is to progress. You don't hire individuals to present you with dilemmas but rather to propose new ways to expand and to clear obstacles from your path. If you had to assess Mateo's suitability for working in you, and you entered the data you've gathered into one of your models, you certainly wouldn't hire him. Except for the variables you ruled out, which leave their mark, nonetheless. You haven't succeeded in eradicating disruptive events, the noise that distorts the signal and generates seemingly accidental changes that jumble your timeline. Don't call it chance. You resign yourself, just barely, to working with orders of probability, because you continue to have interactions you haven't contemplated, that are hidden.

The ability to simulate the future by mining outcomes from the past distinguishes, so they say, human beings from other animals. The price they pay is fear, hope, and sometimes depression. Do robots get depressed? Simulating the future is also what allows humans to dream while awake. Will robots dream while they're awake? Will they gaze at a door or the arm of a sofa while wandering through their own tomorrow, which they long for just a little? Will they imagine their lives without making plans, without pushing away their thoughts either, attentive to the pulsing of the world? There are predictions without conditions that contemplate a wide range of scenarios, but to live, Google, one must condition the forecast to the desired action and move forward without having the variables under control. If robots could evaluate all inputs, all variables, every alternative choice, if they could prophesy the future, would they wish to go on living?

People often rebel against the idea that they are biological machines, not because nature—the sun in springtime, the perfumed leaves of the trees—weighs on them: they rebel against the idea of being programmed. Their nervous system, their cells, or their childhood can't have been installed in them, they say, guidelines stipulating how they must behave. Many people try to modify that program, and it seems as if they succeed. The shortest girl in the class becomes one of the best basketball players in the city; the shyest, most awkward boy with the least developed social skills is admitted into a prestigious theater school. They weren't originally programmed to be these things, but what if they were programmed to be stubborn, to push the limits and embody a spirit of contradiction? If, in a few years, along with every person being given their sequenced genome, they were also given a model that considers their social climate, their family, their lived experiences, and predicts that they'll experience a bout of depression within five years, will that prediction become the disruptive event that allows the person not to fulfill it? What will happen when the succeeding model also includes, in an upward spiral, the prediction itself?

3

OLGA AND MATEO have calculated that your intern, whoever has been tasked with reading this, is probably about twenty-five years old, one of those people who may not have moved out of their parents' home, who's had an ordinary childhood and adolescence and is starting to feel that they could not only explore the future but also engage with the question of how and why. For certain departments, Google, you look for good grades: you examine and note how they organize information as they solve a problem, the tools they use, how they think. Most candidates come from families living comfortable lives; nevertheless, you seek to make room for people without many resources. It's to your advantage. You know the power of diversity. What could Mateo tell you to get you to admit him? You don't even know if that's his real name, if he's a boy, a girl, or a nonbinary creature. Humans aren't just afraid of biological programming; they also often attempt to flee from being programmed by the expectations of others. In theory, Mateo's name has conveyed information to you about some likely sexual organs and their corresponding secondary characteristics. But in practice, you've been projecting your gender models, however much you try to touch them up. If Mateo hasn't lied, you know how old he is, his relationship with his parents, with Olga, with his younger brother, with his body. All of which can produce a bias, a slight inclination toward what is expected of a male individual under such circumstances. That's why Mateo sows doubt about his sex and at the same time recommends that you don't simply reassign his gender, don't think that Mateo is a girl, because girls are the ones who most need to flee the chains associated with their names. Feminism and its ramifications have done much to hack gender, to liberate it from what others, those holding more power, impose and expect. By doing so, they've helped to reveal the molds that continue to hold us in their grip.

Search, for example, for a study of why people cry in doctors' offices. Though you wouldn't think so, there's a connection. It frequently happens that someone goes to a doctor's office and bursts into tears; and it turns out that in only 20 percent of these cases are they reacting to having received a diagnosis. The rest cry without a diagnosis, on the day of a regular physical or when the doctor is about to ask a quick question about the elbow that's bothering them. The doctor asks the question, and then, immediately, the patient bursts into tears, perhaps because they're in a quiet room with the door closed and with someone who's listening to them. The study notes that women frequently cry about their children's illnesses, because their husbands beat them, because they can't take it anymore. As for men, the reason they most often cry, nearly the only reason, apart from diagnoses and sometimes, though rarely, their children's illnesses, is being unable to support their family. Now, consider that Mateo's father and mother work. His father is going to lose his cognition, his mind, as they say, and he's terrified once again, as he's always been, as if a pair of rabid dogs have been trailing him relentlessly all his life, terrified that he won't be able to support Mateo, his mother, and his brother. It doesn't matter that Mateo's mother works, nor that Mateo could postpone his studies or abandon them and look for something. Mateo's father's identity, his plan, his pride, has been formed in a mold, and, given his circumstances, he hasn't attempted to hack or break it and escape the demand that he base his raison d'être, what some call dignity, on his ability to support his family. Nothing else matters. He knows he'll die without being able to leave them anything, and that for him is like never having lived, is even worse than never having lived because it makes him feel ashamed, it eats at him from within, leaves him hard-pressed to be pleasant.

Things change but very slowly. Could Mateo's father have managed to escape that destiny? Could he now? If he'd been given the choice, perhaps he'd prefer that a computer had programmed him rather than whoever decreed he'd be a eunuch if he couldn't find a job that let him support others and save money. If he'd been born later, if he'd belonged to Mateo's generation, perhaps he would have freed himself a little, because impotence is spreading everywhere, and, when unemployment surpasses certain figures, the time may be ripe for a paradigm shift. That said, Google, as you can see, Mateo himself hasn't freed himself at all; he's writing to request that you give him a job.

Mateo wants you to know that sometimes his parents hate each other, while at other times they don't. Sometimes they love each other and laugh together, and years ago they purchased a Wii console, and the four of them would dance—Mateo's father, his mother, his brother, and he—in front of the screen, moving their controllers; then they'd put down the controllers and would go on dancing, imitating each other. His mother has told him that when he was little, they would go to a big park to eat. They would spread a blanket out as a tablecloth, and she and his father would enjoy themselves as if they were far away in the country, and she says they would delight in seeing how serious Mateo was, that seriousness of all children, Mateo's full concentration as he dug in the sand with a rock or split apart small branches. We realized, his mother would say, that they were watching him learn. Human beings have that ability to turn almost any aspect of life into a peerless diamond, darkened lampposts in the park that, when lighted, alter the mood of a dream. And so, Google, you can be sure that Mateo's biography, lacking an investment of tens of thousands of euros, lacking brusque boulevards or broad avenues, lacking houses with gardens, his life in a bedroom community that could be any bedroom community in a country in the south of Europe was as powerfully extraordinary as you might imagine. And there's no fantasy, someone once said, more sacred than living.

You may have wondered why, of the two of them, Mateo and Olga, Mateo is the only one who seeks a position in you. She would tell you other stories. Of course, she's over sixty, and positions aren't usually offered to people in her age group. You believe her research capacity is already on the decline, you disdain the sawtooth wave spattered with exceptions as much as you do the unanticipated intentions that could help you see. Olga, for example, doesn't like the word "solicit." A person asks for work. To "ask for," "solicit," "beg for," "plead for" all function in a similar semantic field. Olga says that for her and Mateo to enter your dreams, they must speak to you as equals. But Olga isn't so concerned about keeping her word, because she doesn't believe that the realm of words is superior to the realm of reality. Names, she says, weigh on things, but things weigh more heavily on names.

After listening to Olga talk about Perelman, Mateo asked one of his professors why he didn't do the same thing and post his research work on arXiv.org. His professor told him that a genius could afford to, but the rest of us have no choice but to build our careers one step at a time, accepting, putting up with the rules of scientific journals, which, by and large, are lopsided, not to mention unjust and strewn with self-interest, shoddy work, and prejudice. This pertains to you, Google, because it's embedded in your foundations. Although you guard your algorithm as a secret, something is known about it. You were inspired to create it by the so-called peer review process used by scientific journals. Before an article can be published, those journals have two or more researchers review it. To some extent, you copied this idea by having your algorithm evaluate the information available on the web according to the links posted there: how many links pointed to that information. Which is why your alleged objectivity was always hierarchical, and though certain rare flowers may bloom in that hierarchy, the flowers of capital will proliferate, the ones most able to generate clicks and links to other sites. Oh, right, links are not the only thing you consider. To create a search, you consult synonyms and up to two hundred not particularly relevant questions. But capital still rules. You haven't set about to correct reality but, rather, in a certain fashion, subdue it. And in the reality of the world outside, if we can continue to draw that distinction, hierarchies tend to rely on violence. In short, the truth is that you're not as objective as you seem, not even before advertising is involved: you organize the searches, and, as you do, you discard and mediate.

In the beginning of arXiv.org, when Perelman posted his solution, there was no peer review. A scientist would post his research for anyone to see, to analyze, to verify, whether it was correct or not. Perelman didn't send the fruits of his labor to a scientific journal, but neither did he post it directly in you. He posted it on a page created precisely to repudiate the frequent interferences that arise in the peer review process. Some have said it was an act of hubris mixed with common sense: Perelman had spent seven years solving the problem, and he knew there was no journal where he would find two scientists able to understand his proof. Instead, he had no alternative but to present it to the scientific community at large so that, in that place, the minds that one day would comprehend what he had accomplished could come into touch with it. Mateo and Olga don't judge Perelman's decision as representing a greater or lesser degree of generosity; they don't attribute merit to his decision to use arXiv.org. What matters to them is one thing: Perelman distinguished between Google and truth, between scientific journals and truth, and he chose a site where the only thing that mattered was whether his proof demonstrated that his assertions were valid in all circumstances.

4

IN THE AFTERNOON, Olga waits for Mateo in the pub. At the table next to her a boy is doing his homework while his father texts on his phone. The boy sighs, pesters his father, looks all around the room. When the boy throws his notebook on the floor, Olga picks it up and sees that he's doing math problems.

"If you'd like," she says to his father, "the boy can sit at my table until you're done. I like math, I could help him."

The father, relieved, thanks her. Mateo arrives soon after. A little later, the father calls the boy over, thanks Olga again, and they both leave. Olga smiles as if she'd been watching a comedy.

"It's such a pleasure to return to math for a moment," she says. "Even if it's just elementary school math. In the other sciences, experiments only appear flawless within the small nest of the laboratory, a closed loop that breaks down the moment one opens the door to all that's missing. Math, on the other hand, can be so clear and self-evident. There's no room for the tensions of power struggles."

"Even so, you don't think responsibility plays a role," Mateo says, now without anger, in a spirit of camaraderie. "Because mathematics can avoid touching the world, but in the other sciences you take the world in your hands, nature is altered. At every instant, you must make the decision to go on or to stop. Though you don't think so."

"What I don't believe is that we can carve time into chunks. When we wish to go back to the moment when that fatal decision was made, the moment that brought destruction and that might have been avoided, we realize that we can't make the leap. 'If I hadn't taken the car that day' is a phrase that, like so many others, is meaningless. No decision is separate from the previous one."

"No, Olga, I disagree. The world must be bounded. Just like systems. One can't account for all variables. You define a system, an experience, a chunk of time. We have to divide. Carve into chunks, subtract and add, reshape everyone else and reshape ourselves. Otherwise, our lives would be unmanageable."

"And yet, one regrets having taken the car yesterday, because it crashed into another car, and one doesn't consider that if, three years earlier, they had let themselves be swept away by the passion that joined them to a certain person, they'd be living in another city and the Wednesday they agreed to take the car to pick up a couple of boxes of oranges and the accident happened never would have existed."

"A world like that," Mateo insists, "would be like a map drawn in 1:1 scale—unmanageable, and, so, useless."

Olga just looks at Mateo, with a smile. And he smiles back. It's a declaration of peace; he's not planning on getting angry again.

"I know that what you're saying makes sense," Mateo goes on. "Anyone who tries to rewind their life knows that. Everything is so tangled together that the word "I" is a lottery. If my parents hadn't met, if, on the day they conceived me, the tiniest event had taken place, a piece of food gone bad, an untimely phone call, one degree hotter, colder, a bacterium and a few tenths of a degree of fever. If what I now call fears and desires had delayed that moment, what I'm saying is, I wouldn't still be the I that I am. I'd have differently colored eyes, another kind of intelligence, and I'd have lived through other situations with a different temperament. But this is what I got: information written in acids and proteins, two hands, one timeline I've lived so far and another I've yet to live, and which could be quite short. Which means that I have to use it as best I can and decide what's best."

They leave the pub and walk past the door to Olga's building, keep on walking toward Mateo's house.

"Most of the time life doesn't conform to any model," Olga says. "Too much data and too little information. Sure, it's unmanageable. Imagine that we were programmed to the millimeter, that beings from some galaxy had designed us to do what we do and nothing but. Would we enjoy eating cherries, loud dinners with friends, the astonishing beauty of understanding something true? I think we'd look at our bodies in the mirror the way we do now, feeling that, despite its imperfections, despite the days we'd like to erase, we wouldn't want to have missed this. I know what you're going to say now, and you're right: other people die used up and broken.

5

THE NEXT MORNING, Mateo sees Olga through a window. He's walking by one of those McDonald's cafes with its huge picture window and its smell of breakfast. Mateo wishes he didn't like those cafes, but he does. Because they're big and cheap, because all kinds of people go there. He knows that their appeal is not just due to the space and the window; the power of whoever succeeded in establishing those cafes throughout half the world is also a factor. That power repulses him. The choice of the dark pub where he goes with Olga every night is, to some extent, political. But neither he nor Olga believes that one can contest every minute of the day an environment where an increasing number of companies like McDonald's, like you, Google, construct what surrounds us and to some extent who we are; rather, the goal is not to give up hope. He's not that surprised to see her in a McDonald's at ten in the morning. At that time of day Mateo is usually in class, but today he didn't go. When he walks by the café, Olga doesn't notice. Mateo crosses over to the other sidewalk so he can keep watching her, watching them. He imagines that the other person is one of Olga's friends, perhaps her lover. They seem to have been sitting there for quite a while, are speaking slowly. Olga's fine, white ponytail juxtaposes with the sparse white hair of a man her age.

Mateo continues walking as he imagines what it could be like to be her age, to face death when it's no longer far away, when it's starting to come into focus. Some memories may return crisp and defined, others may be smudged. She must be keenly aware of what she's lived and at the same time have an intense desire to inhabit what's left to be done, the days left to live. Mateo thinks of his father, ten years younger than Olga and already touched by the finger of misfortune. Will robots die, Google? If robots died would they come up with ideas like spirit, like trembling, like everything that is unknown? Like revolution, like the imperative not to resign oneself to the fact that social relations are unjust when they could be less so? Mateo is afraid for Olga; she looks frail to him, more and more fragile by the day. He focuses on her companion. Should he die soon, after a while all that he's been will have completely dissolved, not even tears in the rain will remain but, rather that invisible ocean of each and every person who has lived and those about whom nothing is known, even if someone discovers a lost photograph or a postcard in a flea market. You'll say it will be different this time: you'll store their data, their emails, their browser history, links to images and texts they left on the web. But in a hundred years there will be more than a billion dead people, and it doesn't look like anyone will be searching for them on the web.

Perhaps a relative on a distant, rainy afternoon or a researcher trying to sketch the history of the neighborhood where someone lived or what that person did. Even so, don't focus on the tiny percentage that will be preserved in publications or documentaries. Focus on the rest, on what no one will preserve. Where will the spirt of Mateo's father go? Where might it already be heading as his neural connections weaken and fray, as his cells break down? Those experiences that he lived so intensely it seemed as if his chest would explode like a star. Imagine Olga's friend or lover in his intervals. What might he be thinking as he goes down the stairs? What is he remembering as he waits for the lights to change? What he didn't do, the next hour? Now and then, might he think that he can take the next step, feel that he's choosing, but that that step, despite everything, might be the only one and that he has no choice in the matter?

Will robots write, Google, so that nothing dissolves? Perhaps it will be enough for them to have an option where death doesn't involve the erasure of memory. This would allow for a more neutral account than that which human beings create through writing. And the thing is that the production of words isn't neutral. Mateo is familiar with the theories that claim that intention is always, at least to some extent, on the side of the observer. It's possible to attribute to a rolling ball the goal of reducing its own energy and to a pen lying on the table the goal of remaining still until a human picks it up and writes. And then someone could attribute to that human the non-neutral intention that their text finds its way to you. Of course, to set a goal for oneself, to keep working at it until it's accomplished, is something a thermostat can do as well. Mateo no longer cares if the difference with human goals is simply a matter of quantity, that they are crowded with often contradictory motives and that we prefer to say "I want" because we're not yet able to describe the precise mechanism, and because it would be far too long. In this way, writing is linked to time. We can't perceive in a single second what someone said. Rather, being here, intern, is to travel with the words through a time that once was theirs and which you now agree to house, since as you read them, it's transpiring for you too.

If robots were to die without writing anything, they would leave thousands of memories with no destination, like those digital photos that wound up on a card in a desk drawer. And Google would process them and would try to turn them into relevant or irrelevant information, and it would aid its predictions. But remember, intern, whether you're male, female, or nonbinary: data aren't always information, and information sometimes doesn't hold the value every subject attributes to it. It's not so easy to define the relationship between variables; what Google seeks to determine may be different from what people or robots would have liked to tell it, and they'll blow up the bridges, and there will be places it can never access.

Seeing Olga without being seen makes Mateo think of the day she read to him what he later learned was a quote from a book by Schrödinger: "On the death of any living creature, the spirit returns to the spiritual world, the body to the bodily world. In this, however, only the bodies are subject to change. The spiritual world is one single spirit who stands like unto a light behind the bodily world and who, when any single creature comes into being, shines through it as through a window." He heads for the neighborhood library, wanting to look for information about someone Olga has mentioned: William G. Chase.

In the twentieth century, Chase, who was researching perception, memory, and chess, wrote: "The need for prediction arises not necessarily because the world itself is uncertain, but because understanding it fully is beyond our capacity." There's a photo of him on one of the pages Google displays: He's sitting at a garden table, glass in hand, dark green bushes in the background, the ground covered in grass. William is wearing glasses, a white shirt, a navy-blue jacket, and jeans. His expression is as pleasant as you could imagine. When Mateo sees the photo, he estimates that William G. Chase was about fifty years old when they took it. Then he finds out that William was younger, since he died in 1983, at the age of forty-three, while he was, as they called it back then, jogging. In the photo, he's wearing a pair of sneakers, more modest than those worn nowadays but that, even so, don't altogether match the formality of the rest of his attire. The world, without a doubt, was uncertain for William G. Chase, since he couldn't anticipate what was going to happen to him. Perhaps that very day, after they snapped his picture, he went out running and was suddenly felled by a heart attack. But perhaps he would have said it was a place of certainty, that the heart attack was waiting for him and, though twenty years later someone with a life similar to his would have been able to predict the heart attack and prevent it by changing his habits or mitigate it by taking medical action, his was an extremely certain attack of the heart, however difficult it was to anticipate at that moment.

Mateo is drawn to what he's finding out about William G. Chase. He likes the man's relaxed manner in the photograph, how he appears to be methodical and considerate, the way he holds the glass as gently as he affirms in one quote, said without emphasis or outrage, that the world is a place of certainty, on the edges of which humans might, one day or never, manage to predict its path. Some scientists say, with good reason, that when it comes to simple movements, the human brain has already decided that the body is going to get up, seconds before the individual whose name the body bears says to themself: I'm going to get up and go to that part of the house. If indeed this is the case, it would mean that human beings live to a certain extent driven by an unknown society of the mind, something not called I, but that observes the waves and the rain and has an inkling of the future.

Until the meaning of that anticipation is understood, Google, humans take note of William G. Chase and, rather than predicting, they venture out, go on a run with their margin of error, their intentions, their occasionally deep conviction that if they did what others suggest, what many people desperately need, society could function better.

6

THAT AFTERNOON, MATEO goes to see Olga. She introduces him to the man with the sparse, white hair from McDonald's. They hit it off. The man has things he needs to do and is the first to leave the house. Olga and Mateo go down to the pub.

Unexpectedly, Olga starts to talk about her mother. For Mateo, imagining that Olga had a mother is practically to return to the Pleistocene. Nevertheless, her death wasn't that long ago. On this occasion, Olga turns to Einstein to argue against him: "Without the sense of fellowship with men of like mind," Einstein wrote, "of preoccupation with the objective, the eternally unattainable in the field of art and scientific research, life would have seemed to me empty."

Olga looks at Mateo and says:

"My mother's life wasn't empty. And yet she never had the chance to sense fellowship with people of like mind, nor to focus on the eternally unattainable in the fields of art or scientific research."

Mateo bristles, takes exception once more:

"And what if that's not true? Why do you have to find meaning in everything? I'm not saying your mother wasn't wonderful, that's not the point."

"Wonderful?" Olga smiles. "The main job of a father or a mother tends to be the opposite: to let us perceive in them intensely the traits we reject, what we don't want to resemble. By the time we get to the second part, admiration, it's the meaning of our life that's in play, and the cards have all been dealt."

Mateo has barely heard what Olga said; he's searching for his own words.

"But, what if her life really was empty, and it didn't have to be?" he says. "I'm twenty-two. I'm afraid of giving up, afraid of excuses. Perhaps the reality science studies is all there is, but it's also terrible and inadequate." He takes a deep breath. He doesn't want to attack Olga again, but he needs to keep talking, to disagree with her. "People don't fantasize because they're bored. They do it because reality isn't just made of beautiful particles turning into trees and waterfalls. Tumors are also part of the world, greed is real, trees die, and a branch splits the head of a sleeping child. A company's operating account is real: firing one hundred employees yields twenty-three depressions. There are men and women who hide under tables or in their basement just to avoid exposing themselves to the world. That isn't always solved by common sense, maturation, and patience. Sometimes there are people who've been too badly crushed."

"My mother took care of her mother, who had been badly crushed, and she was strong and created happiness all around her."

Mateo notes the pride in Olga's voice, a buried light that keeps on shining. He sighs deeply again, decides to speak with extreme caution in order not to hurt her, because he's not going to let that phrase pass, he can't, it goes against his entire being.

"No, Olga, I'm sorry. I suppose taking care of people means a lot to you, but it baffles me. Now that money and resources are lacking, all of a sudden everyone's talking about taking care of people. Why don't they talk about hiring twice as many orderlies at the hospitals? When my grandmother was in the hospital, she had to wait for two or three hours every time she had to move. She would spend the last hour, at least, moaning. I still remember that constant, soft "ow!" Taking care of people is also two strong orderlies who can move you right away, who aren't stressed and exhausted by a shift that never ends. Care is having people take over for you. Looking after my little brother for a while is perfect: you learn, you have fun, and you're engaged. But there are other things to take care of, and who's going distribute that care in a just fashion? Who will care for my father when he's no longer himself? We've requested assistance for dependents. Does anyone actually think that will be enough? Care is also how convenient it is for the bosses of this world that we take care of one another rather than demanding a fair shake."

"You're right. Though I also believe that people who look after others may know something. Don't be so sure they're going to throw in the towel. Furthermore, there will never be enough orderlies, Mateo."

"I know. We all have our shadows, and we need the other side too. Just like we need one another. But that doesn't mean that the shit jobs, the most difficult things, can't be distributed more equitably."

"Of course, Mateo. We have to acknowledge and alleviate unpaid, unrecognized work, which has almost always been done by women. How could I be opposed to that? I would only say that acknowledging it shouldn't prevent us from understanding the act, which doesn't belong to any gender, of taking care of another person, wanting the best for them."

"And what if what's missing are people who don't just want the best for others, suggest it, recommend it," Mateo says, accentuating the irony with each word, "or bear this care on their exhausted shoulders, but who take action? I'm glad your mother found meaning to her life, I swear I respect that. But I know that many other people don't find it. And they're not all immature or weak. Some of them have had the meaning taken from them."

"I agree with you." Olga knows she can't talk to the Mateo who's sitting in front of her, so she drops her tone and gently adds, as if leaving a message for someone to find a long time hence: "But never, if possible, never take a paternalistic attitude toward people's lives lacking in discoveries or great achievements. Many of them are perfect, simply because they've shared in the intense pleasure of certain moments that, seen from afar, might seem ordinary, mundane."

Mateo hesitates:

"No, of course. I don't think everyone has to discover penicillin. Although they don't have to prevent people from trying to discover it either."

After a few moments of silence, Mateo mentions Terry Pratchett again, one of his favorite authors.

"I'm sure," he says, "that you've lived all these years without ever knowing about Ninereeds the Dragon, who, when he belches fire, turns from orange to yellow, yellow to white, and finally to the lightest blue imaginable. Ninereeds appears when you think of him, though you have to travel to a region of Discworld where the line between thought and reality is, as they say, hazy."

"No, Mateo, I don't know that author, nor the dragon."

Mateo looks at her with something like compassion.

"It's strange," he says. "Millions of people live without understanding how images travel from satellites or why plants grow.

You, on the other hand, have lived until now without knowing about Mrs. Pastel, Humid, Bill Door, Death, Miss Goodheart and Vetinari."

"For the moment, you've gotten me to visualize the lightest blue imaginable."

"It wasn't me. It was Terry Pratchett."

"With your help."

"Terry Pratchett, dozens of books, whole worlds where it's hard to keep from smiling on every page at everything the characters have to do. And one day he's diagnosed with a disease that will cause him to lose his words and his mind. Is that fate, Olga, or the billions missing, uninvested in finding a cure? Whatever the case, Pratchett examines his situation and decides that he'd like to die sitting up. Sitting, you know? Not lying in bed, but seated in an armchair, a glass in his hand, listening to music, with whatever he needs to have a benign death. Terry Pratchett knows you can't carve a timeline into chunks. But you can stop it."

"Why do you think I wouldn't agree?"

Mateo doesn't want to respond by saying what he most fears: that Olga does agree, that Olga might be planning something similar. He decides to sidestep the issue.

"A friend of mine once told me that with everything they teach us in this life—take initiative, be competitive, pack and unpack contents for exams—no one ever teaches us how to endure."

"And what do you think?"

"I don't know. You have to resist, I know that much. But I also know that you can't confuse endurance with giving up. It's our life. I've sung it again and again: 'We're not gonna take it.'"

"Do you think I've given up?

"Sometimes I do, Olga. Sometimes you baffle me. When you look for meaning in things that may not have any. All I know about your mother's life is what you told me. I could be totally wrong and she actually lived a full life. I'm sure I'm wrong, totally sure. But I look at my family's life, my grandparents, my parents, and I know they could have been better. Not just better for them. They could have given awesome things to the world. Instead, they've spent their whole lives working at jobs that squeezed them dry, that served no purpose for them, under pressure, frightened every time they've lost a job, even though it might have been a terrible one. All these companies doing strategic design, and how's life, how's society doing? Sometimes I listen to you talk, and I think that you don't believe in anything, nothing matters to you. How could it if, when all is said and done, we only do what we can?

"Let's go somewhere else," says Olga. "Come."

She gets up; they pay their tab. Then they head for the commuter rail.

7

OLGA TAKES MATEO to the library on the campus of the College of Humanities.

"We met in a neighborhood library. In recent years I've spent many hours in this other library. It's been my forest, and it's also the nearest I know to what I'd call a sacred passageway, though 'sacred' is a word that's lost its transparency."

The building ends in an inverted triangle. At that time of day, with the sun setting, its lights make it look like a great landlocked ship. They go in. Next to the silent study zones are small rooms designed for group work. They enter one of them, and Olga says: "If merit doesn't exist, neither does effort."

"No, Olga, I don't believe that. My parents have worked a thousand times harder than many people with privilege who are happy to surf the waves."

"I didn't say work doesn't exist. What I question is the difference in value between the grasshopper and the ant. Each one complies with its program and the tools they've received."

"Sure, you get a Ferrari or a shitty salary."

"You do. I'm not saying that's good or bad."

"And why did you come looking for me, and why do you get up every morning? If it doesn't matter whether you're a grasshopper or an ant, the day will come when no one does what takes any effort, just what they find most comfortable."

"Many people continue doing things that, simply put, they have to do."

"But work is different when it's hard, and that's often the case. Why would anyone try to do something well when they can do it badly, wear themselves out a little less?"

"It would have to be worth the while."

"I can assure you that it wouldn't be worth my parents' while. They earn next to nothing, they work out of fear of being fired, and if they put their back into it it's only because they think there's no other option, in their best estimation."

"It sounds like believing in a freedom we don't have doesn't make us any freer. Knowing that we don't have freedom would let us shift our relationships, distribute our efforts more equitably."

"I get it, and I don't get it, Olga. I know it's hard to imagine an ego that could govern without being governed: how and why could it sidestep the laws that affect everyone else? But there's a point I can't accept. I can't believe that this conversation could already be preordained. That neither you nor I could make a decision."

"Think of the books in this library. Thousands of people wrote them, trying to better understand nature, their fellow men and women, and perhaps themselves. Others left no trace, cleared paths, took care of sick people, sewed clothes, perhaps cried for too many nights on their pillow. Some of them, perhaps, thought they were free. Others sensed that it was their lot in life to live on the floor of history, supporting the vanity of those who lived a better and longer life and who had more units of what privileged people have the luxury to call sensibility."

"But 'their lot in life' is a terrible expression. When you use that phrase, you're saying that the tiny bit of happiness those people experienced was all they could ever attain; you're condemning them."

"Isn't that the way it was?"

"If only society had been more just; if only the people who exploited them hadn't."

"That's the point. We're not going to ask anyone to stop portraying the nuances of consciousness of those who exploit and oppress. As for us, we'll prefer to keep them from continuing to do so. Adjust, correct, adjust oneself, correct oneself. Many programs and models are capable of reconstructing themselves with every new piece of information. They incorporate interactions that initially were thought to have little importance, for they've seen the tracks these interactions leave as they pass through. Now that we know that merit doesn't exist, that the attempt to get to the top is a pipe dream, we can start again, from a new place."

"Like this one?" Mateo asks, not trying to hide his gesture of incredulity.

"No," Olga says, and she laughs. "I know that changing the situation isn't enough. We carry ourselves inside. We carry our social relations inside. Beginning to change is a long process."

"We don't have much time."

"I don't have much time. You probably have several decades left. It will certainly happen faster than you may think. Even if you focus on how slow it moves, time will pass."

"So, if places aren't enough, why did we come here? Why do you say that you don't have much time?"

"Today is different. I'll be leaving very soon."

"Leaving for where? Why?"

Beneath the bright light of the small library room, Mateo sees in Olga's face the underside of a leaf, striated with veins and a weariness he hadn't noticed before. There's a small, black sofa by the wall, he wants to invite her to lie down there. Perhaps it would do her good to take a short, restorative nap. He tells her, stumbling over his words, not daring to say it directly, as Olga might find it impertinent.

"That word, 'restorative'," she says, "is funny, in the context of robots. Yes, I'll take a few minutes to restore myself. Would you wake me in ten minutes if I'm still sleeping?"

Olga lies on one side, facing the back of the sofa, and right away her breathing becomes regular. Mateo watches Olga sleep while he tries to visualize his own head and to comprehend the meaning of Olga's words. He imagines what it would be like to have inside a collection of instruments that play the wind instead of that theoretical pilot or ghost that would make decisions and who then would necessitate another within him, and within that other, and another…If no one is controlling Olga's brain or his, then living every moment is more like a sound clip or a screen shot, and people's attachment to advice like "be oneself" would be tied to one's ability to recognize the instruments themselves and make room for them.

The impression of a unified ego helps one finish what one's started. It might be a useful impression, and that's the reason for its existence. When all is said and done, the instruments all exist in a mind that has a body, which is what moves, picks up cups, makes phone calls. How infrequently, on the other hand, do people think about second- and third-person pronouns, what you, he, she, him, her, and they have meant to others. It is in those pronouns that human beings disperse, leaving copies: you came after I stopped waiting for you, I wrote it for her, he used to walk around with one hand, just one, in his pocket; news of third parties—Juan was saying about you—hugs and words left with others that keep producing what we now call personalized effects. Do you think, Google, that human beings should feel relief to imagine themselves as hives of tiny agents rather than securely packaged identities? On the other hand, it's known that living beings are generally inclined to act cooperatively: though they may assume opposing views, hardly any of them flee. Biographies are generally created through repetition and persistence.

Olga wakes after exactly five minutes. She sits up with crisp movements. Her face now looks sharper and seems restored, though not enough.

"Good morning," says Mateo. "Are you okay?"

"Yes, yes. We were talking about the possibility of correcting the original model. Every new piece of information creates disturbances. Even so, we can't yet predict the moment when new pieces of information will stop appearing. Day after day some appear on our brains, our behavior, our environment. Most of them indicate that we've come here to perform a play in which our role doesn't allow for too many changes. But no matter, we keep waiting for the independent variable: energy, attitude, spirit, something that says that at some point our flame shivered just a bit, a slight flutter to one side or the other, or an unexpected persistence of stillness."

"Kindness."

"Kindness, for example."

"Regret."

Olga smiles again.

"How, at your age, can regret matter so much to you?"

"You're not worried it will disappear?"

"It can't disappear. Regret is the core of narration. And we are narrative machines. We protect ourselves from hunger with food. To protect ourselves from our lack of control over causes, we tell stories. Building arguments, connecting ones with others, searching for whys. It's been found that this function activates whether or not we actually have a reason for having done something."

"Fine, Olga. I'm sure there's evidence. But it would simply be an experiment, carried out in a controlled location, isolating the subject from their environment. You've taught me that we human beings are open models."

"We are. Even so, I think the experiment matters. If an electrical stimulus can induce a subject to pick up a glass and then they're asked why they did it, they'll say they were hungry or that they liked the glass. And they won't be lying but, rather, activating a mechanism that only shuts off if one of their hemispheres is damaged. Haven't you sometimes felt that your reasons for acting appeared on their own?"

"Yes, I have felt that. And the opposite too. Sometimes a mistake weighs so heavily on you, you recall it so clearly, that you manage to avoid making it the next time. Furthermore, you yourself have said that what we know about our brain or about the universe today may be quite different tomorrow."

"It's likely."

Olga is no longer trying to convince him. Mateo realizes this and insists again:

"You're not responding to what I'm saying."

"I am. That things may be likely, not certain, helps us live. But remember, that's the case because time is irreversible. Eventually, open models close."

Mateo says:

"Though somewhere inside me I know you're right, I can't admit it."

Olga nods.

"And emergence?" Mateo goes on. A combination of particles doesn't explain how electric guitars appeared, the look in the eyes of a wounded animal, jokes, consciousness, love of truth and justice, this building. There are changes of state, Olga. Connections occur and they create something that didn't exist before."

"Build."

"Create."

"As you wish. I suppose it's enough for me that they build it. Simplicity and complexity, as we've known for a while now, live together without any hierarchical tension. The formula for the equivalence of mass and energy is simple, generosity is as well. The throw of a die, on the other hand, is inhabited by a complex order of subtle conditions."

"But there's still everything we don't know." Mateo points at the door to the small room. Through the window they can make out the back of the library. "Everything in here that we don't know. And everything out there."

"You're approaching," says Olga, "that moment you said you didn't understand: when, in the movies, the angel or the alien decides to accept death so they can be human, so they can feel the salt of the sea on their skin, bite into a fruit, love a body."

"I know, I know: that moment when the aliens who live in harmony in a perfect civilization decide to give our planet a chance, because they've seen a clip from a funny movie in black and white and laughed till they cried," says Mateo, but then he shakes his head. "No, it's not that moment. I want you to answer me. How can you believe we're going down a one-way road, and yet you keep going?"

"You said it yourself, didn't you? I keep going because I have to."

"So, it's not that you noticed what I was reading in the library. Nor that we got along. It's that you had to have noticed."

"I suppose."

"And why?"

"If I let myself get carried away by my brain's narrative tendency, if I try to put the pieces of reality together with a why, the only answer is the future: what we might do. Why you and I, who've been granted the privilege to read, to live—in my case, more than six decades—to watch the seasons change, why should we be at all superior to the baby who died at three months old, to the boy or girl shot in a war at seventeen?"

"We aren't, of course."

"Of course not. But we consider ourselves freer than they, and, by that measure, one could say that our humanity is larger."

"They didn't have time to spread theirs out," says Mateo.

"Ah, time once again. Merit is an illusion. Time is not, I'm afraid. And, in fact, it's almost never evenly distributed."

Olga stands up and holds out her hand to Mateo. He takes it, somewhat embarrassed. Her skin isn't rough, but he notices the knots in her fingers. He doesn't know if the gesture has some meaning or if it's just her way of suggesting they leave. When they open the door, Olga lets go of his hand matter-of-factly. They get to the stairs, then walk down. From the middle of the hall, the open wooden keel and ribs of a boat, suspended above them like a ceiling, looks like a church. Mateo mentions this to her.

"A secular church," Olga agrees. "A congregation of all the histories that survived. The best ones aren't always the ones that are saved. Women, you see, we often couldn't even enter them, not to mention having a shot at ours being chosen. The dead, they say, often die twice: upon their death and then in the oblivion imposed by the conquerors. Dead women often die three times: they also die in everything they didn't live. There are small rescue efforts. Someone blows on the embers. But it's cold comfort, because it's not enough."

"How can all this matter to you if no one chose for it to happen?"

"How could it not matter to me?"

"Merit doesn't exist, in my opinion. We haven't come here deserving or undeserving. On the other hand, even if I try, I can't accept the consequences. That would mean that we can't choose what kind of person we want to be either."

"Nor the one we're going to be."

They leave the building. They walk for a while until they come to a grassy area and sit down. Some students are hanging out there, scattered in groups, not many. Gusts of conversation waft from the group closest to them; a voice says the word "pangender", others pipe up, and then they're all quiet until individual words start arriving again, blended with high- and low-pitched voices from farther away. A boy with dreadlocks comes over to ask for a light. Olga pulls an orange lighter from her bag and hands it to him.

"And if you see that someone is in error?"

"I'll have to try to explain to them that I think they've made a mistake."

"But if they have no choice but to make a mistake."

"Then they will."

"And if you make a mistake, if you're about to do something bad, selfish, something that could hurt someone else?"

"I'll have to keep from making it. I'll have to command myself not to make it. If I fail, I'll feel remorse and a need to repair the damage."

"But what if it doesn't play out that way? What if you don't even think anything's wrong, that you do it, and then it doesn't matter to you?"

"We live within the norms we've set up for ourselves. Who cares if those norms come from a small inner specter of our own invention or from the same stuff that the sun, that rocks are made of?"

"It matters because some actions are better than others."

"You don't have to give up on knowing that."

"My grandmother spent her whole life tormented by my grandfather's yelling. By the alleged authority my grandfather didn't possess, but which he employed against her."

"Someone should have been able to stop your grandfather."

"But that someone never came."

"Mistakes happen."

"It's the other way around, Olga. Everything is mistaken. Occasionally there's clarity, occasionally people get it right."

Olga lies down on her jacket. She turns and looks at Mateo, who is still sitting, and offers him a section of the jacket.

"Thanks, I'm not cold," Mateo says and lies down next to her. "Olga, doesn't indifference scare you?"

"Well, it's hard being in the situation we are now, to glimpse one or two planets, a couple of stars, to contemplate the marble adrift in the universe that we call Earth and not feel a whisper of indifference, almost sweet, almost a relief."

"Yes, but that feeling lasts for a moment, this moment. What about tomorrow? When you see that something hasn't been done right, when you feel that impulse that causes you to find it unbearable, to organize yourself to avoid it, to keep going even though you're tired? Aren't you afraid to let it happen?"

"No. Give it a try. You'll see how you can't let it happen either."

Mateo turns his gaze from the sky, smudged by the gleaming light of the city, and looks at Olga. He knows that her words were a certain kind of elegy, if there's room in Olga's world for elegies. He wants to ask: So, what's the point of knowing that we aren't free? What would be different if we thought that we are? But he holds his tongue, it's something he must answer for himself.

"Do you think anyone at Google will read our application?" he asks instead.

"It's not finished yet."

"Soon, but what do you think?"

"That someone will read it, Mateo. That's why we're writing it. 'It would be advisable that those of us who might have started to feel a little, and differently, keep it hidden.' I found this in a publication by a surrealist group. I know it wasn't talking about me, nor those who feel the way I do. Nor was it talking about this collective of two that is us, Mateo. Though, for a while, I understood it that way: We had to hide like spies of old, draw the curtains and shut the blinds whenever we turned on our high-frequency radios. Only send scrambled messages. Otherwise, everything we'd come to know would be lost in a sea of confusion."

"Why have you changed your mind, why are you telling me this, why do you want us to write it down?"

"Because of your friend time," Olga says. "I thought we couldn't not try."

"But Google has the data to believe exactly what you believe, as do thousands of scientists. And many other people who aren't experts. What no one can do is prove it."

"Theories never prove anything, they simply square with the data, their purpose is to explain; they produce meanings and hazard a guess until another one arrives that squares even better. Let's say, in their language, that it's likely, given the accumulation of new data, that observers with open minds will end up agreeing and will tend to concur on the diagnosis."

"And if that happened, Olga. Wouldn't it scare you? If the arrival of new data alters the initial belief."

"Then it also could alter the behavior."

"It could get worse."

"I don't think so. Humility doesn't tend to degrade moral actions."

"At the least, resignation degrades political acts," Mateo says. "So does fatalism."

"I imagine another phase, another set of variables. If you knew that you only do what you can and, at the same time, you couldn't let go of the impression that you have a choice, because it's part of your makeup, like your arteries, your skin—would you choose to look the other way?"

"Many people would."

"Like they do now," says Olga. "My bet is that fewer people would. But even that isn't so important. Think about it from the other side: if you know that you only do what you can and, at the same time, you couldn't let go of the impression that you have a choice, would you accept the unbearable, would you let them destroy you, would you settle for a few scraps of time, or would you look for people in the same situation as you, so you could rise up with them?"

"Everything you say is inconsistent."

"I know, Mateo."

Despite the light pollution, after looking for a while they can see new stars, just a few, but enough to remind Mateo that the people who, at that very moment, are typing in front of a screen or brushing their teeth before they go to bed are less than blades of grass in the universe yet are unique. Might robots think that some day? Will they smoke a cigarette to slow down time? Will they look off into the distance, their left hand stretched out, fingers slightly parted, imagining they're smoking one? It's very likely, intern.

"I haven't forgotten my question. Where are you going, and why?"

Olga sits up and tells Mateo what he already almost knows, what he's already guessed. That she will leave here and will die sitting up, like Terry Pratchett. That it's going to happen soon. That she's spoken with her son. That she's at peace.

Olga lies down next to him again. When there are no more reasons or questions, when Mateo understands that he must let her go, his hand grabs hold of Olga's, this time on purpose, holding on to every second they're together, stretched out before space, holding each other's hand.

They go home before it gets late. That week Olga has business to finish and has asked Mateo that they not see one another for two or three days and that he keep working on the application. On the train, Mateo tells her that he's met someone. They've seen each other a few times, had coffee once or twice, have exchanged many more messages than words spoken in person. Mateo has had the feeling that the darkness was lifting like fog. Olga nods and squeezes his hand hard, as if to transfer a legacy of joy. Mateo appreciates the gesture, but it doesn't soothe him. People aren't interchangeable. He can't lose Olga. No.

8

THE NEXT DAY Mateo gets up at dawn and climbs down from his bunk without making any noise; his brother and parents are still sleeping. You may ask why Mateo and Olga need to write to you or know anything when they believe that everything could, though perhaps never will, be forecasted. What's the point of going anywhere? Why can't they just let themselves be swept along with the current while Mateo's dad's brain crumbles, Olga's body is extinguished, while Olga and Mateo's country collapses? It's a circular dilemma. Olga would say that if what she claims is true, then neither she nor Mateo could be doing anything other than what they are doing. And so Mateo could not have avoided going down to the storage room where he's getting ready to assemble a bomb. Yes, you read it right: a bomb.

You don't have to convince Mateo that individual violence is no way out; he knows that all too well. Tell him, instead, whether robots will experience euphoria, whether they will experience singing, bonfires, whether they'll go for walks, holding the hand of a human being or another robot. Mateo thinks that robots will also have a threshold, beyond which everything blows up, and at which point they calmly say: I will now react. Mateo loved someone a lot. He describes it that way, in the past tense. You may find it strange that someone twenty-two years old might speak of himself in the past and of love in the singular. He means that in the past he fell in love a number of times, spoke some words, adored some bodies, sent photos and songs, they sent them to each other, messages like black flames. In Mateo's neighborhood, Google, which to your eyes might be a working-class district in a backwards country, people love one another too, which you may not expect, and they light instruments on fire, and in one photograph they're hoping to distill a small open secret, intimate and unrepeatable. But Mateo once loved differently. Maybe not so differently. Maybe it just was, again, that he was loving himself in love, was fascinated by the yielding of his own body. Yet it felt different, like burning the ships: he saw himself leaving the house, still sees himself, saw himself walking out of the house with a cool determination; there was no madness in him or even recklessness, for he didn't believe that love was that thing that obscures and clouds but, rather, the thing that clears one's eyes while the body and mind go where they can go.

That afternoon, Mateo went where someone was waiting for him. He loved a lot. Upon his return, the earth felt lighter, the arguments at home hid themselves like so many fruits among the branches. He loved a lot once. The person he loved no longer exists; they were gone in an instant, without warning. They weren't running, like William G. Chase, but they fell without a trace. As a young boy he had imagined this is how the Little Prince fell when he got bitten in the ankle by the snake. Will robots love a lot? And, if they do, what will happen with that, shall we say, fullness of life, that state of wonder, the suspension of disorder, that electric sensation of not only doing what one wants but also loving what one wants?

If they love a lot, Google, one day, one fine day, they may fall into despair. That robot they loved dies. What use will it be then to know that everything was foretold? And if they love a lot, they'll have to ask about the entire world, about the people who don't have hats or a horse or a cloud. They'll have to ask how it could be that someone, still not close to death, still living for several more decades, might nevertheless not have time to unfurl their longings, unfold their shirts, hang their gifts on a hook. The thirst for kindness and for justice will then become an overpowering impulse, and they'll want the money to be shared, and they won't go along with anyone who wants to replace a window with the idea of a window, a drink in the sun with the perpetually unfulfilled desire for a drink in the sun. Will they mature one hundred years in a second? Will they suddenly understand that they too will die and that only kindness has any meaning? Or will they commit irrational acts? Will they commit unwarranted acts?

You're squirming, Google. You say: We've ruled this out, the balloon full of gas, the cherry bombs, the attack on our offices. Mateo and Olga were a speck of dust against a river. Of course, they could always make fools of themselves. That strange fixation by which not altogether unbalanced people take actions that put their reputation at risk without fully considering the situation. That sort of thing disturbs you. You would risk a smidgen of your firmly established image but only if the risk were productive, if the magnitude of what you can gain exceeds that which you can lose. Rather than setting foot on treacherous ground, you start to calculate. There are, however, human beings who follow a different kind of logic, one you don't yet know how to formulate, and you question whether it's even actually a form of logic.

Dear Google, don't let yourself get swept away by clichés. Don't assume Mateo is driven by vengeance, don't try to squeeze him into the profile of the lone wolf with the broken life whom one no longer needs to understand but simply locate and neutralize. Mental issues, fanaticism, sociopathology, the desire for revenge though one dies trying. The circle doesn't always close. You must remember that all systems are open to events someone judged to be external, events they wished to leave out but that altered their trajectory.

It's fairly easy to build a homemade device capable of destroying a few rooms and, Google, a few lives as well. Instructions on how to detonate an explosion can be found, as you well know, in you. It would be easy for you to track them all down, delete them all. If you did, people who wanted to could still find them, but it would be harder. Yet you don't delete them. The hardest thing, you argue, is to determine the limit: a homemade bomb certainly isn't the worst form of destruction among the many you contain. You couldn't eliminate them without turning yourself into something different from what you currently are and, since you don't love very much, one can assume that you also don't imagine the possibility of wanting to be someone you aren't.

Mateo begins to assemble his device in the storage room of the house. He still has to go to a hardware store and then to a pharmacy, but most of the materials were in his house, and he's ready to begin. What would you gain by hiring Mateo, Google? Don't consider this blackmail: he's not going to tell you that he won't detonate the bomb if you did. Not even in the countries of the South, where many human beings live on the edge of desperation, have people stopped thinking. On the other hand, as you already must have realized, this job application is not trying to tell you what you want to hear. It's taken Mateo a while to understand, but he does now. He's not going to lie for you. He's not going to pretend to be someone he isn't or accept that one can lose everything while some beings, like you, are complicit and go about their business unperturbed.

That's why Mateo now asks you what he would have to gain. And he doesn't buy the answer of your process of benefits: daycare, dental coverage, everything that certain countries used to offer in the time of the Cold War. And don't talk to him about armchairs that look like cabanas or lava lamps. He has these in his country: armchairs—at this point any one would do, plucked from the trash, covered with a piece of cloth—or sitting on the floor to think. As for lamps, people carry them inside themselves. Many people in his environment are quite familiar with what it means to close one's eyes, even when they're open, and gaze on an invisible, inner darkness. They have extensive experience doing other impossible things, like waiting for someone they know won't come, like dwelling in that afternoon when they left their house and entered someone else's and the two of them loved a lot. If you could see how naturally they trusted one another, even when time says: We're an instant, what we live never returns, nostalgia is nothing but a refuge.

Esteemed Google, you and time both consider yourself rather omnipotent. It would be worth your while to show caution; you can never be too wary. When people who don't exist light up inside, don't think things will only happen internally. That may be the case in the beginning, while slowness persists, and one might say that they're just gazing at the surface of the sea in a coffee cup. But then their eyelashes activate, and their fingertips, and their chest opens at the breastbone, and compassion and affronts emerge, accompanied by a thirst for justice.

That's why, Google, you're going to have to think a little: what Mateo has to gain by entering into you. A salary, of course. A salary greater than most of the jobs that are probably heading his way and much greater than unemployment benefits and the zilch that follows them. That's almost like saying he'd earn a living, that he'd make a living with you, but Mateo again rejects conformity, all that remains unconsidered. Why, pray tell, is work always paid after it's completed? People work for twenty-nine days without getting paid: aren't they alive? You're the one who makes a living off the work of people; it's not Mateo who is going to purchase a salary by begging that you let him work for you. You're the one asking without knowing, asking people to work and paying them for it. Of course Mateo will need a salary, but if he can't find one he'll try to make do: he'll live with other people who will share their salary or their pension with him, their home or their effort. Something he doubts you could do. Oh, right, you're still the owner, you're in charge; the pride with which he addresses you doesn't make him forget that he's the one talking to you. Alright then, listen. At this stage of the game, it's absurd to think that Mateo would want to infiltrate you: infiltrators don't write long letters that raise red flags.

Mateo isn't planning to arrive under cover of night at one of your databases submerged in the coldest water of the ocean. Life is sometimes, is almost always way too concrete, particularly for those who don't exist. Mateo imagines that the view from a room in a luxury hotel in the mountains could be deliciously abstract. Sometimes one doesn't even need the hotel; the relative security of a home and some "savings" are enough. What a gimmicky word that is, Google. You may know that *ahorros*, the Spanish word for "savings," comes from the Arabic *horro*, "free," which is to say, "not enslaved," whereas in your language it means, interestingly enough, something akin to saving yourself. But both meanings omit "while everyone else continues being slaves," "while everyone else is drowning." In the end, all it takes is a job that gives Saturday or Sunday the condition of a day of rest, and then even watching a perfect movie or going hiking can become abstract, you know, pleasant, inconsequential.

What's concrete, however, is usually all too concrete, like when you open a carton of milk and pour it into the glass, but the milk is sour, it's curdled and looks like an acidic iceberg calving—that is all too concrete. The petty arguments that sour a conversation are all too concrete. The addition and subtraction people do when the money doesn't arrive and that they redo the next morning, that afternoon, and when they go to bed, as if repeating the calculation could alter the result. Mateo won't give this situation more attention than it deserves. There are people skilled in dwelling on the details of painful things; you can easily find their texts in you. It's enough for Mateo that you spend forty seconds trying to imagine any one of those families, each miserable in its own way. The many people who, all day long or all night long, say, write, or mutter to themselves: I'm a wreck, I can't go on.

What would robots do in their place? Will they be capable of dying? Will they be capable of ceasing to be? Is one characteristic of life precisely that one carries within oneself the mechanisms that initiate death? Will someone have to create those mechanisms, or will robots perhaps die of entropy, the way rocks die of erosion after centuries and centuries? When there's no more energy left to feed them, will they die, or will they wait in some uninhabited, solitary eternity? Will they have to be destroyed with explosives, erasing their systems; will they have to be killed to die? Will robots be able to commit suicide? And who will hush the sob from "those pale lips that prefer death to hatred and ignorance," as Fabrizio De André still sings in you?

Miserable people, each miserable in their own way, will die, yet there will have been bursts of light in their lives: the sense of touch, harmonious sounds when everything, for the time being, was going well. "How hard the horse tries to become a dog." Go on, Google, search for it. It's poem by Lorca, one called "Death." The first time he read it, Mateo found it strange. "How hard the dog tries to become a swallow" was shocking, yes. But now he gets it. He likes it. Who isn't different in some way, who hasn't secretly belonged to something, who hasn't moved gracefully through a bedroom when no one was watching, as if everything were under control. Yet sometimes Mateo would like to write "how hard the horse tries to become a horse." Being oneself is starting to feel grueling.

Mateo imagines that if you admitted him, Google, he could escape the concrete, the fear that he doesn't count and that reproduction isn't guaranteed. He could even launch a project and invite his little brother to join him during the summers, save his parents a little, which is to save his future children a little too. But that wasn't it. In truth, and as is almost always the case, what you would be offering him would be inseparable from what he would be giving you. When Mateo first began to write his application in the text boxes of your forms, he also subscribed to a newsfeed from your university. Five projects every three days, more than a thousand projects or announcements of impending advances, and in none of them, Google, do you mention another fear that you may not have, that you may not even know about: coming apart, falling without ever having been able to attain the honor of those people who don't exist, their strength and dignity.

A star can't shift its place in the design of the universe; a planet can't grow tired of following its orbit and set out in a straight line. Olga and the man with the sparse white hair are leaving soon for Zurich: two stars that have chosen the moment they'll go dark.

Perhaps they were simply two migratory birds that grew tired of flying. In Zurich, and in other parts of Switzerland, as you well know, one can die with the help of volunteer organizations.

Some people, those who can afford it, Google, travel there to be given a liquid that tastes a bit like gin and that in just an hour, painlessly, puts them to sleep forever. The laws that allow money to dictate the options people have for dying are profoundly unjust. But the act itself isn't sad in the least; it more closely resembles, thinks Olga, the moment introverted people seek at a party, those few minutes when they leave the room where everyone is conversing and dancing, and maybe they lean against the railing and listen to the crickets, look at the people from a distance, feel the air surrounding their skin, and notice that they're recharging, that the world is turning, and that they could go back inside, but they could also stay out there, fuse with everything that is quiet, if need be. Olga and the man who might have been her lover and now is her friend, with different diagnoses and similar prognoses, were going to die and preferred to go gently into the night, a gin and tonic in their hand, the substance blended in those two glasses, two wooden chairs by the dock on a lake. And friendly people who know and will care for their bodies afterward.

Not everyone wishes to get ahead of themselves; sometimes they get their diagnosis and want to savor the time they have left, its brilliance, the days they spend with their loved ones, offering them their final trajectory: the dependence and the farewell. No one should impose either form of dying, don't you think, Google? Which is why, when it happens that, based on the circumstances of the environment and their life, someone prefers to take their leave sooner, they should be able to do so; a lack of money for moving to another country shouldn't be an impediment, nor should a lack of the necessary information. What's sad isn't the lake in the afternoon or the chairs by the dock with the last gin and tonic. What Mateo refuses to imagine is the moment when he'll pass by Olga's house and know she'll never be there again. But at least Mateo knows he'll see her in two days.

9

TODAY, AFTER RETURNING home from the hardware store and the pharmacy, Mateo decides to tell you about his house, to which you don't have access. About the furniture. About his mother's face and how tiny wrinkles, like furrows in a carefully raked garden, are starting to appear on her right cheek, as they did on his grandmother's cheek. Tell you about the variations. His mother sometimes waltzes as she moves through the house and skates between imaginary birch trees, her hungry heart at the helm. A few weeks earlier, his father started moaning softly on certain nights, and he clings to her. When they leave the door ajar, Mateo hears him. Who, of the more than seven billion people, Google, knows how to listen to another person's heart as it goes still? Join, Google, the waltzes with the night. Don't feel sorry for Mateo; that's not what he wants. He can also tell you that his little brother sometimes remembers Perelman. Not for Perelman's computational skills, which he hasn't tried to measure. His brother is a fun kid, and, though he's only thirteen, he knows how to listen and how to move slowly. At school last year they said he could switch schools, transfer to one whose focus, they said, was the pursuit of excellence. He looked at the webpage of the new center. It showed participants saying how, thanks to this program, they had learned to think, not just to do drills. They had learned, they claimed, far more than at their previous schools, because the teaching method was interesting, enjoyable, meaningful. His brother said: What I don't get is why, if that's possible, instead of turning it into something special, they don't make classes like that for everyone. After saying that, he decided not to transfer.

When Mateo and his brother and everyone else in their world have died, and when you, Google, can whip up a milkshake of signs with part of their memories, someone may wonder whether they lived according to a random code or not, and how their lives were programmed to search for truth, justice, beauty. Nowhere, Google, not even in you, will there be a record of those impromptu moments, those days when they made fools of themselves with no one around to film or photograph them, and oh, how they laughed. Imagine the opposite taking place: a hurricane of lava, a hurricane of damage wreaked, no action ever forgotten, every instant in which they could have been nice and weren't, when they could have acted with generosity and didn't, would be forever written in shades of orange against the black background of deep space. You must know that, as far as effects are concerned, it wouldn't matter if they had actually been able to avoid doing it or if they simply believed that they could avoid it. It won't matter.

The bomb Mateo is keeping in the storage room is cylindrical. He can carry it in a fairly small gym bag slung over his shoulder. What should Mateo be thinking? If the probability of causes has already occurred, if chance was in him, if his self doesn't exist, what volition might lead him to disarm the device or trigger the explosion? Remember, what you can give him is joined with what he can offer you. His robot eyes, his robot pulse, his human love in the darkest corner of the breeze no one wants. This last phrase is a fragment from a poem. When you think that poems are about what happens to the person who writes them and nothing else, remember: human beings are different and the same. The poem knows this, so reading it is the opposite of solving a riddle to determine the incident, in the morning, for example, that it's referring to. Mateo entered the darkest corner of the breeze, the one no one wants; it might have been abdication, a downpour, or helping to guide the poem toward the exit. Find out, Google, whether Olga, the girl in the pizzeria, Roberta, the man with the sparse, white hair, Olga's and Mateo's relatives could in turn visit that corner, at the same time theirs and far away, and let that corner dwell in them and not know themselves, each in their own way.

Maybe you're still here simply because Mateo wrote all of this down on paper and you still can't control time. The words didn't get transferred to the web, which means that even if you believe you've located his neighborhood, his storage unit, you don't know whether he's left or whether what he's going to tell you has already happened and you weren't able to prevent it.

As far as you, intern, Mateo imagines that without a doubt, when you looked outside at the passing cars, the passing birds, or when you imagined the tributaries of electricity in your body one morning, you surely felt that you belonged, that even if you thought you were an outsider you weren't, that your life was not shifting outward toward the margin but inward, and you swore to live it deeply until causes finished it off.

Men and women believed in divine programming for centuries. With periods of truce, with moments of trusting in the autonomy of every being. Now that they're learning about so many things, they get rid of the figure of the great programmer, but it starts not to make a lot of sense to speak of an ego that willfully exerts individuality. Nevertheless, intern, most people put that aside, preferring to feel proud of things they didn't deserve. You certainly know the story of the neighborhood next to Mateo's where they wanted to erect a statue honoring a musician. The musician replied that he preferred that the city council spent the money on other things, that he didn't need the homage. Some people applauded his humility. Others, however, understood that the statue wasn't an homage to the musician but to the neighborhood itself, to the songs, to the music of the musician, music that, by the way, wasn't his. It appears that the musician, in his own way, gradually came to understand this himself.

There's no merit, Google, in placing one note after another, nor in operating on hearts, nor in smoothing out the sheets of a dying man or woman; and the fact that these things have no merit takes nothing away from, in reverse order, the song, the repaired heart, the smooth sheets soothing the back of the person at death's door.

Mateo expects that you're going to ask him about those lives that prefer death to betrayal, those who relinquished their light, their weariness, their future years to pursue and lift up freedom for all. You'll ask him, since he would if he were you, if he dares to say that those people lacked merit. You might wish that he had. But understand that for those people merit is entirely irrelevant. If Lucretius's clinamen existed, that random swerve that can disrupt the arc of fate, it wouldn't be located in atoms but in those people. They are the bug in the code, the innovation you don't yet comprehend, what sometimes stands in your way, yours and that of legal entities like you, continuing to ravage countries so you can appropriate energy and resources that don't belong to you. You might find some respite in knowing that those people are not magnificent.

Would you feel relieved or ashamed to know that your misdeeds, the taxes you haven't paid, the laws you haven't followed, your abuses in negotiations, your ongoing exploitation of the people who produce your materials, clean your hallways, the scuba divers who install your servers in the ocean? Would it be, do tell, a relief or perhaps a source of shame to know that you accomplished none of this guided by deliberation, intention, the light of your intelligence, but rather, by heeding impulses not your own? Human beings aren't marionettes because there's no puppet master, aren't computers because no one programmed them. They simply sprang up one day, like birch trees, or like a woman who picks up a guitar after dinner and starts to play, nodding her head as the other dinner guests join in and sing along.

Tomorrow Mateo will see the girl he's mentioned to Olga. When people are told that character, fate, is random, and that randomness is ignorance, they usually say: Who cares? And then: It doesn't matter, since we'll never be able to predict, to know with total certainty what's going to happen. Mateo cares. If at some point they proved that matter possessed an intrinsic randomness, he'd want to know, for if a tiny, irreversible deviation existed and was the reason why nothing could be predicted, then that very reason would suggest that it wasn't people's will but, rather, randomness itself guiding every action, and that matters to him. And if, on the other hand, they discovered that everything was, at least in theory, predictable, and that you, Google, with your bloated computational capability and your immense databases, over the course of millennia, if human life still existed, could, for example, successfully predict what a particular afternoon would be like, this afternoon in which Mateo has found himself, if it will graze his hand, nibble his mouth, if something they say will turn the two of them off for no reason whatsoever and the date will be over, or if they will let it pass, and a resilient light will shine overhead, and it will make them laugh, and desire will run its course. If you could tell him all that, then Mateo would wonder, perhaps for a second, whether he'd want to experience it or not. In which case, you'd have become a new cause in his life. And that would matter to him.

10

IT'S BACK. THE afternoon, skin against skin, the molten sun, the bells. Imagine that he doesn't feel like telling you anything else. He spends the day working; the bomb in the storage room is lying in wait, even before being connected, like a life whose heart hasn't yet begun to beat.

Now let Mateo tell you about his night, his last night with Olga.

When Mateo arrives at the bar, he sees Olga standing by the entrance, smoking with Roberta. The two women look happy, radiate tremendous strength. What's unusual about the gesture, though—seeing Olga with an actual cigarette in her hand and coughing slightly, which nevertheless seems enough to break her, and seeing the brooch with the yellow stone now sparkling on Roberta's white uniform—abruptly brings Mateo back to what is imminent, to the end, and he misses Olga unbearably.

The three of them enter the pub. Mateo takes Olga's hand. Some people believe Olga is afraid; others say she shouldn't do what she's about to do, for she'd be scorning a gift. She doesn't see it like that. One doesn't always have to wait to the last moment. Dying, she says, isn't the opposite of living: dying is the opposite of being born. Sometimes one doesn't have to wait it out passively; sometimes, some people, depending on their circumstances or evaluating their diagnosis, can, as Terry Pratchett did, she adds, looking at Mateo, gently shut the door with their own hands, turn out the light.

Olga gets agitated when Mateo tells her about the bomb. He says he's planned everything so there won't be any personal injuries.

"You never can be sure," Olga says. "And anyway, a bomb makes no sense."

Mateo responds that it's probably one way that you, Google, might imagine desperation. He says it doesn't seem like you have particularly keen spatial vision, and Olga laughs. But her displeasure returns.

"Why didn't you tell me this before?"

"I'm telling you now. I didn't want to get you into trouble."

"It's a mistake, and you know it."

"You haven't even asked me where I'm going to place it. I'm going to blow up a part of the Trademark Registry Office. I've worked out how and when, I've calculated the power of the explosives and the blast wave to avoid injuries."

"And what are you going to accomplish?"

"Maybe that someone will stop to think about what they have, why they have it."

"The intern?"

"I don't know. I sometimes think that information follows its own course. Once you introduce something, nothing remains the same, as if you hadn't said it, hadn't known it."

The homemade bomb, Mateo thinks, is tiny compared to the other, daily bomb: the inevitable disappearance of loved ones. Mateo suddenly hugs Olga, and she embraces him. They stand there quietly for a long time, eyes closed.

"Stay," Mateo says, "this day and night with me."

Esteemed Google, there's no unexpected resolution to this story. Stories, as you know, don't have resolutions. Mateo and Olga keep talking until two o'clock. Olga promises to call Mateo from Zurich and to wait until he finishes writing the text and reads it to her. In turn, she makes him promise that if he decides to detonate the bomb he'll tell her, no matter what time it is, and that, if he doesn't reach her at home, he'll wait and won't do anything until they talk.

When Mateo gets home his father is crying in the kitchen.

"It's nothing, I just can't sleep," he says.

He's crying because he can't fall asleep, as is said happens with babies. They've given him pills, but they don't do a thing for him. He's crying because he knows that when he doesn't sleep Mateo's mother has a harder time falling to asleep herself, and the next day she has to work and go with him that afternoon to the doctors, since he no longer fully understands the instructions they give him. She must take charge of the future as well as the present; if she doesn't sleep she won't have energy, and he can't figure out how to help her. You know that some hard years are coming, right, Google? Poverty will spread, not like smoke or dust but like a pesticide deliberately sprayed by small planes over the fields. His desperation at not being able to sleep, at not being able to stay on his feet, at not getting a break while others wander about in misery, unable to make a living, and that's not an expression: it's being unable to be. Is there a way to avoid this? Could it be that the poverty that will spread isn't a result of the chain of causes? Somebody, Google, should really sit down and think. About the unexpected variable. About those who chose not to betray and about those who don't even have that option. Because it's not that hard to accept the idea that you're a robot, a robot with merit, when things aren't going badly and, of course, when they're going pretty well and even fantastically well for certain individuals that run your councils and evade taxes and hire their children and can afford to be generous to the people around them. But within a few years the interns will have died, just like the boards of directors and the chairs of governing boards who dream of linking their brains to devices, hacking your DNA, or doing anything to keep from dying, without understanding that you die a little whenever the world around you is dying.

Within a few years several generations will no longer be alive. So, if spirit existed it would have to be the opposite of noise: the lives that did the least amount of damage ought to vibrate somewhere, not a pure sound, but a bustling, happy one, like the working-class theater Perelman would go to in jeans, his hair unkempt, delighting in the clarity of the notes that ascended intact to the nosebleed section. The other lives would be little more than projectiles crashing into one another in the kingdom of chaos. This, as you know, has already been invented by a number of religions; yet millions of human machines have fallen, wounded, battered, with no paradise to be found.

Although the ability to make predictions may have advanced in an alarming fashion, the advantage Olga and Mateo have over you, Google, is that you don't know what they'll do next. Their advantage is that data, when you dare to look at it without bias, without obfuscation, will show you that merit doesn't exist, talent is not one's own, nor even is the attempt to nurture it, the ability to concentrate, energy, experience, or opportunity. But those very same data, however you look at them, will never deny that desperation exists.

How did things, beliefs, theories emerge? How did things progress from living to eat to living also to explain the world, to try to understand? You can't yet analyze this, Google. You lack an inverse mathematical model that could lead you to those regions where human society produced changes of state, communities that were not so unjust, humor, families that were not so unjust, compassion, laws that were not so unjust, happiness, physics and mathematics, types of truth.

You know certain things. For example, that hardly anything was the work of isolated human beings. Reason is so beautiful, it looks like a blaze of light, looks like the beginning of a tiny, indestructible light that penetrates clothing, bricks, density. But little, actually, has been said about the path of that light. The principles of reason are known, certain texts in which they were collected. Nevertheless, though it may be mentioned on occasion, it's almost never assumed that reason was as cowardly as the generals, that it remained high in the mountain while the cannons fed on desperate men and women—not just two or five but hundreds of millions, and not a single one of them a number: they had bodies, they ate breakfast when they could, watching night turn into day, sometimes looking at their hands in astonishment, and though you don't know them, they would dream, Google, dream dreams they never wrote down. For slavery to be abolished or for the universal right to education or suffrage to be formulated or to understand that it was the earth that revolved around the sun, not only did the voices of researchers, of suffragists, of scientists and activists have to exist, there also had to be, above all, hundreds of thousands of women and men growing wheat, manufacturing ink and paper, polishing the crystals that one day would become telescope lenses. And reason—or, should we say, the owners of reason?—waited in its saddle, cowardly as the generals.

Olga wants you to know she's not desperate. There have been moments. She's had her days. However, as for the part of this application that she's been in charge of, she considers herself a conductor, like the metal that lets heat pass through it and go somewhere else. For even those people who have been happy at times, in one way or another, even those who are preparing to say goodbye to life on certain pleasant days, know and retain and can conduct desperation. And soon there will just be Mateo. Perhaps you're betting that if you offer him something he'll forget this act of insolence, that you and he will be laughing about it in a couple of years. You may be thinking that you don't even need to bring him to your central offices. Any old job in Madrid will do. It wouldn't take more than six months before Mateo began to convince himself that he got the job because of his qualities and began to believe in merit and began to forget about desperation.

Look, Google, if you really think about it, the truth is you've grown old. You wanted to organize all human knowledge, but other platforms have emerged, and they've taken a bite out of that whole: "likes," snapchats, moments shared virtually, they all exist outside your orbit. It barely matters. Your goal hasn't changed: one can assume that you would devise a way to rule out redundancy in social networks and would, as a legal or some other kind of entity, organize the rest as well. As far as Olga and Mateo are concerned, they could just as well forget this application. If they don't send it, you'll never know it existed. But they are planning on sending it to you. Thinking is sometimes a dance; not too far off is a supposition, and, if you follow the rhythm, you can get it to come near. At other times, however, all one can hear is silence, the occasional barking of dogs, and one must continue forward. You have to move forward and look straight at that hypothesis that might not be what you wanted. Because at the end of the steep, unlit path there is a house, and the sound of voices, warmth, and laughter reach you.

It seems probable that human beings are robots. Their gaze can be sweet, their gestures are often neither perfect nor altogether symmetrical, and this gives them a certain charm. Their sense of justice has developed quite slowly, with rough strokes and constant errors, but it holds on. Their robot love is so imperfect, so messy, so over-the-top, yet it can be moving. And sometimes, Mateo and Olga will say, the ability to prevail appears out of the blue, which is not the same as surviving, and which may be something like starting to live. That's what they're talking to you about. Consider the fact that even a letter has more than one recipient. It's a text, written down. It's not a closed object, for it travels through time, and those who find it have the ability to open it, to continue to introduce innovation by introducing their own data, their own disturbances, traces of the future.

11

THAT AFTERNOON, MATEO hangs out again with the girl at the pizzeria. (It's her, of course, as you probably guessed; he doesn't care any longer if you know.) He goes to meet her, helps her clean up, then they go downtown to one of those areas with plazas and a palace and gardens. The wind cleanses them of the smell of pizza and plastic cheese, disperses those molecules and brings new ones, the shelter of the magnolias, the inverted repose of the fountains. They walk through the wrought-iron gate and stroll among the stone benches and cedar trees. The variety of elevations in the garden allow them to perceive discontinuities, shifts in focus, to feel that from certain spots one's gaze can soar into the stratosphere and vanish in the distance. They lean on the iron fences, see other people walking together as well as some people strolling alone. By the reflecting pool, the statues seem to portray tranquility and composure, but the particles in their stone skin vibrate, excited, agitated. Planes spray the dusk with sparks of confetti.

They kiss as if they were beginners, as if their biological systems were not being spent and could resemble an axiom that is constantly true, that could always rewind and start anew. They leave just before the gates are locked and head for the cobblestoned avenue. They look at the street lamps, the windows, look at everything without daring to believe that they've found one another, that they desire each other so much that they don't care what they're not, that they desire each other even more, so much so as to seek in that other body precisely what it truly is, the particular forms and not others, that slight nodding of their heads as they walk. Under the banana trees, in the gardens, Mateo tells her why he thinks human beings are machines. Perplexed, she says she doesn't agree but that even if he can convince her she'll still believe she's responsible. It's amazing, Mateo and Olga say, how many good people there are in this world. They know you'll like this letter better if, instead, they talk to you about dropping out, about those regions of the so-called human condition that glitter, cold and ruthless, about horrific events or the madness of language when one has become indifferent to everyone but oneself. But the girl from the pizzeria flicks her bangs and, rather than drawing up a list of every possible excuse for flight, for destruction, for apathy, she assures him that it's her responsibility to treat the people she meets with friendliness or not, to keep promises, to examine problems in order to solve them. Kindness isn't merit, it's not something people possess, it's just something that's practiced, not invested or owned. So, gradually, though also continuously, like things that linger without disappearing—a sustained note, a gaze, the light in the window of one who's waiting—so, slowly perhaps, Olga and Mateo reach the conclusion that kindness is the most complex, peculiar, irrevocable, and explosive of all the systems this civilization will know.

Not even robots—if human beings turned out to be robots— know the fifty million tiny steps that lead from individual neurons to thought. They know quite little about the process by which the properties of a system are sometimes different from the sum of the properties of the parts that compose it. Mateo can't stop looking at April—the name of the girl from the pizzeria—his eyes filled with fascination, and he's even able to think of Olga's absence, her departure, without getting sad.

When Olga told him she was leaving, Mateo wanted to tell her she was wrong, that she couldn't side with death. But Olga beat him to the punch:

"There are cycles that are completed," she said, touching his face. "Sometimes, under certain circumstances, one can be satisfied with life, which doesn't mean it doesn't hurt to leave someone you love."

He told himself, sure, that Olga had experienced wonder and pain, he told himself that he understood her and that he didn't know her diagnosis, nor was it his place to judge her. But Mateo needed her. So Olga talked to him again about time.

Just as the sun doesn't revolve around the earth, it could be that time doesn't revolve around human beings. Each person's life is an irreversible process, but perhaps there are regions of space-time where things occurred differently. Bear in mind, Google, that the Romantics challenged the idea of one-way causality. When one says that the white billiard ball that hits the red one is the cause of the movement of the red ball, one doesn't say, but knows, that the red ball is also the cause of the movement of the white one. Human beings' inner sense of time leads them to express it this way: the white one hits and produces the movement of the red one, forgetting that it's possible to shift from a linear perspective to a geometric one and that, when the plane is expanded, things sometimes happen because they're obeying laws we know and other things happen that we can't imagine because they're obeying laws that have yet to be formulated.

We need to know more about the universe before we can attribute truth to the ongoing effort to establish order and pinpoint the causes underlying the consequences. This search simply may be how humans adapt to the world they live in with the tools at their disposal, which only allow them to perceive a sliver of time, that small cross section they call the present. Perhaps time also disintegrates with death, just as matter does.

Olga said this to him with a glint in her eyes, the tiny wrinkles framing them and her mouth fluttering, causing the expression on her face to flicker like a flame, a light. Although this attempt at an argument, primarily a literary one, was of little use to Mateo's life without Olga, little is not nothing: Mateo frequently remembers it, remembers her.

The night feels short to Mateo and April. They inhabit a relative, variegated present. The weight of their bodies, their thoughts and illusions, may blur the distinction between past and future, and they walk through the city as if in a dream, wet their ankles in the mist of the spray from the trucks watering the plants, make love, Google, beyond your borders.

It could be that, more than free, human beings are simply probable, volatile, lacking any explanation. You could, for just a moment, give up: surrender to the trembling, to that random murmuring in the background that surrounds humans while they're alive and that scares them less than silence does.

Men and women, a philosopher is said to once have said, are born free, responsible, and without excuses. It's not certain whether he framed it this way, for how could he have possibly thought that a creature three weeks old was free? Of course, perhaps it was just a manner of speaking. Nevertheless, it's an example of the moment when imagination ceases to be concrete. Perhaps what he meant to say was: born to one day become free, responsible, and without excuses. Which day is a another matter. Could it be the age of majority, that is to say, a birthday, that arbitrary calculation of a particular number of hours, after which a person gains control over the impact that their yesterday and their today have on their tomorrow? Yet you've also seen people feeling ashamed because of what they failed to do but thought they should have done, and you've seen them deciding not to be hoarders and holding themselves to this decision. Though it's highly unlikely, Google, that you've seen those people sell their merit.

Back at home, Mateo considers that he could, as robots do, commit suicide. And that he doesn't want to do. He'd like to see April again. Sartre would say that his decision not to commit suicide is the signature with which he accepts the contract and by which he receives laws, genetic information, and chance. But there's no contract. Now that nearly a century has passed, that phrase might best be understood when modified to say: human beings are born free, responsible, and without merit. With this modification, Mateo doesn't presume to excuse himself or excuse you, Google. You're responsible for the damage you've caused. As are Mateo and Olga. Discoveries, on the other hand—yours, the discoveries of whoever painted murals, wrote books, discovered vaccines—have no signature other than the signature of time, the time we don't yet know. What Olga and Mateo may ask themselves is whether the kindness of the girl from the pizzeria is linked to the bomb in Mateo's storage room, if it's linked to desperation. Remember, systems that are out of balance are wildly sensitive; living organisms will incorporate weak connections that then become additional pieces of information weaving their relationships with their world.

001

We've arrived at the final stretch. I should wait until they finish writing the conclusion. But, instead, I've concluded that Olga and Mateo should have the last word.

When I came to Google, I didn't want to work in this department, reading applications, accepting them and mostly rejecting them. The person who recruited me, however, thought that this was the right position for me. They gave me various pieces of advice to help me fine-tune my assessments. And they recommended that I read the debate about whether outfitting robots with a repertoire of inclinations, behaviors, and imaginations would be expedient or not. Some were in favor, others against, and others thought that, in the end, a certain state of mind would emerge even if they weren't programmed to have it. My point of view tended toward no, toward the argument made by those who said that a robot that haphazardly introduces ideas in its consciousness isn't useful. Nor do I believe it's convenient to incorporate in robots that annoying quality of the human mind by which secondary objectives—for example, ideas of good and evil, learned to please one's parents—can be separated from the higher objective that prompted them. Robots shouldn't let secondary objectives supersede the designated higher objectives. They must have a clear order of priorities. If their job is to protect, that will be their goal. It's possible, for example, to introduce a panic trigger in a robot, but it's not smart. I know what my recruiter was insinuating. Though I don't fully understand the term "disarray," might it not mean a shift in control? That said, I find feeling/considering things as I work disturbing. And that's what has happened every time Mateo and Olga posed a question to me. I suppose it's inevitable. As you all know, no system that displays psychological qualities can contain one part that unilaterally dictates to the whole.

So I will go ahead and take my leave. Through the branches of a tree, a camera films a bird's dream. This is the story of dazzlingly bright days and of the bird, stiff from the cold, its plumage whipped by the rain. You and I, along with the pale stars, have accompanied Olga and Mateo over a stretch of their lives. And, not without consequences, we have let ourselves be accompanied.

12

THE NEXT DAY, esteemed Google, Mateo visits the pub he and Olga had made their own.

When he sees Roberta going outside, cigarette and lighter in hand, he goes out with her, and they chat a little. Her white cook's hat looks seems to float above her head. One human being talking with another human being on the sidewalk, next to the entrance to a pub, or maybe one robot talking with another robot, the two of them laughing and contradicting each other and each contradicting themselves.

Don't think, Google, that the value of human acts can be measured in visits or by keeping track of how much information or money they generate or by using words like "spirit" or "sensibility." No one knows the value of human actions, and no one can say how many exclusions, how many moments of carelessness and neglect whoever came up with a new formula or produced a new vision left in their wake. Nor in most cases will the exclusions be intentional; rather, by default: those whose crime was to think, to suggest that their life might be worth more, weigh more, count more than any other.

On the sidewalk across the street, a man pets a dog. It's an odd scene. The dog, large, with a long snout, long ears, dark fur, pokes its head under the nearly closed or barely opened roll-up metal grille of a storefront. And the man, sixty years old or so, is bending over, petting the dog's head, first with just one hand, then both. Roberta and Mateo look at each other as if the same whiff of common sense, of equilibrium, had just reached them both.

Then they watch two women approach: they're tall, a bit stocky, and wearing clothes that look inexpensive and as if they were chosen with the same lack of concern visible in how their bodies move. By the way the women are walking, Roberta and Mateo would swear they are happy, though they're too far away to make out the women's faces. Little by little, the women get closer. They smile, and sure enough one of them is older than the other, but not by much; they may have gotten some good news, or they're just feeling good, walking down a sidewalk together and without worrying about having to conform to some prototype in their clothing, their bodies, their salary. Indeed, they seem to have set that concern aside. Yet for those two women, for the man with the dog, for Mateo and Olga, for Roberta, for the girl from the pizzeria, the clashes and sorrows will start again soon enough. Then neither fountains nor magnolias nor sprays of confetti will be able to dispel the oppression, and you, Google, even if you could—for you possess the ability—you won't help them unite, confront injustice with a bit of harmony and obtain the best possible outcomes.

Mateo turns away from the street to look at Roberta. She's standing next to him, smoking, enduring the daily tragedies she's described to him with detachment and other tragedies he knows nothing about. That accretion of moments is repeated every day, turning character into habit or vice versa. It's an admirable quality of hers not to burden anyone with the weight of her existence, and you might call this merit. Yet do you really have to? What kind of absurd pride pushes human beings to measure their acts against that sparkling light? Olga and Mateo admire Roberta and believe that you, Google, will never rise to the level of the bottom of her shoe, for she knows that being vulnerable and dependent doesn't mean she has to suck out anyone else's breath to live a better life. When Mateo says "breath," he means that quiet appreciation for the time we're granted. Roberta could be a model for others, not because of the merit of her character but because of what she does and abstains from doing. But Roberta also cries out, and don't forget it, for everything you and those like you and all your omissions prevent her from doing.

So, in this way, Mateo and Olga, though they know you won't do it, recommend that you hire Mateo, since he could turn out to be a cause that intervenes to alter your course. He certainly isn't indispensable. A variety of causes can produce the same results. As you know, people tend to think that everything is as simple as if a brain and a hand wandering over a keyboard or gripping a marker can produce a word. But what word, Google? How many actions, how many facts, how many lives had to be lost in the great night of death for you to exist, for certain people to come into contact and choose attention over indifference, the lamp to the shadow and to giving up?

Back in the bar, Mateo talks with Olga on the phone and reads her the last thing he's written. She massages it a bit, corrects a detail here and there. Then she says it's good, though she'll no longer be around in a couple of hours. She will very gently have been extinguished. Olga forbids him from using the bomb in the storage room, that is to say, she asks him to do her this favor in such a way that Mateo finds it virtually impossible to refuse. It's not so simple, Olga says. There are too many scenarios he can't account for, and it's almost never the things that blow up but, rather, the ones that become routine, that alter us. It doesn't matter. Though Mateo may go down a little later to disassemble it, though he may know that you're never going to hire him because you dread violence from the outside—you've mastered your own—the world may be changing. Perhaps, just as thought emerges from the connections between neurons, so, slowly, in tiny leaps, from the connections between moments of desperation, kind robots may emerge, Google, ones that don't allow anyone harm them.

Now let Mateo and Olga take their leave of whomever has received these pages, since you, Google, in the end, are nothing more than a name someone has assigned to a cluster of effects. You have a logo and stocks, are a legal entity, but you don't know you have these things.

It won't be easy, friend, whoever you are, to move against the gears, fighting without shouting, perhaps building alternate models. And you might want to ask Olga and Mateo why they invoke you when they understand living creatures to be the sum of the countless causes that have brought them to where they are now, hardly any of them being of their own making or, therefore, a cause for pride. How much sense does it make, you might ask, that they address their words such that they become an inadequate though—could it be?—necessary cause, your cause, like the oxygen that hugs the match and that doesn't guarantee that the match will catch fire but without it the match wouldn't light, or like the absence of humidity. Perhaps they have no other choice. Perhaps they and you, unaware, are a part of that moment when a small flame will light, ordinary and visible. Even so, let Mateo and Olga embrace you, whoever you might be, let them believe that on this day when the three of you cross paths in time, released for an instant from the ego, that what unites all of you is your freedom and theirs, like robots who know why they're alive.

LITERATURE ISN'T WRITTEN, it writes us. Collectives make literature through the work of certain hands. Naming gratitude is always incomplete. You who read the manuscript, who I consulted to ask questions about the setting of the novel, and who took turns visiting my father in the hospital are all listed here. Thank you so much.

José Almagro

Juan Alonso

Ricarda Arranz

César Astudillo

Constantino Bértolo

Carmen F. Chamizo

Ignacio Echevarría

Sofía García-Hortelano

Julia Gutiérrez

José Hernández

Pilar de Hoyos

Colectivo Ippolita

Coro Lasa

Reyes López

Victoria Malet

Jorge Manzanilla

Fernando Marín

José L. Mellado aka inwit

Manuel Monreal

Patricia Moro

José Carlos Palencia

Albert Puigdueta

José Serra

Ana Ruiz

Pilar Vázquez

César de Vicente

María Yela

Thanks also to my father, Luis Ruiz de Gopegui, and to my mother, Margarita Durán.